Emma Moss ☆

GIRLS CAN VLOG

Amazing Abby
Drama Queen

MACMILLAN CHILDREN'S BOOKS

First published 2016 by Macmillan Children's Books
an imprint of Pan Macmillan
20 New Wharf Road, London N1 9RR
Associated companies throughout the world
www.panmacmillan.com

ISBN 978-1-5098-1738-2

Based on an original concept by Ingrid Selberg
Copyright © Ingrid Selberg Consulting Limited and Emma Young 2016

The right of Ingrid Selberg and Emma Young to be identified as the
authors of this work has been asserted by them in
accordance with the Copyright, Designs and Patents Act 1988.

Page 79 © Marcin Krzyzak/Shutterstock.com

3 5 7 9 8 6 4 2

A CIP catalogue record for this book is available from
the British Library.

Design by Lizzy Laczynska
Printed and bound by CPI Group (UK) Ltd, Croydon CR0 4YY

For three amazing girls – Evie, Abigail and Olivia –
better known as Evablia! Thanks for the inspiration! X

Chapter One

To: TheRealRedVelvet100@gmail.com

From: amazingabby@abbys_world.com

Hi Tiffany,

It felt weird typing 'Hi, Red Velvet' so I'm using your real name instead of your vlogging name. Is that OK? It's also kind of weird – in a nice way – calling you Tiffany, just casually like we're mates! Meeting you at Springdale fundraiser last week was literally the best day of my life, and I wanted to say a huge sparkly THANK YOU for giving my friends and me tips about our YouTube channel. We are insanely proud to have launched Girls

Can Vlog and we've got our first planning meeting soon. Can't wait to get the whole thing up and running. It was super nice of you to share your email address and I was wondering if . . . ☺ you could maybe mentor me and give me advice for the channel in the future?

But I get that you have nearly twelve million subscribers to keep entertained, so I totally understand if you don't have time. ☺

Anyway, it would be fabulous to hear from you, even if it's just leaving a comment if you get the chance to watch any more of our vlogs. I hope your perfume launch went well – obvs I'll be asking for a bottle of Velvet Touch for Christmas. I bet it smells INCREDIBLE!

Abby XOXOXO

'I'm home!' shouted Abby, slinging her school bag on the kitchen counter and pouring herself a glass of Coke. 'You here, Josh?'

Silence.

And no blaring music from his bedroom either.

Her older brother attended the same school as her, but they often went entire days without crossing paths – and for now she was glad that loudmouth ball of energy was out of the way.

Her mum had said she was working late tonight, which meant that Abby had the house to herself. Result! She needed to prepare for the Girls Can Vlog meeting she was hosting for her friends, and she wanted everything to go perfectly. Lucy, Hermione and Jessie had gone home to change (school uniform was a big no-no when vlogging) and they would arrive soon.

'Hi, Weenie!' she cried, scooping up the little cream pug who had zoomed over to greet her, and giving him a kiss on his funny squashed face. 'What a day! I missed you. Did you miss me when you went for your walk with

Susie?' She giggled as he licked her face, grimacing at the smell of dog-food breath. Susie the dog walker came to take Weenie to the park every day when Abby and Josh were at school and their mum was at work.

Still clutching the pug, Abby jogged upstairs and cast off her uniform, shedding with it the memories of a long and stressful day at school.

Wow, that felt good, she thought, kicking her wardrobe door shut so that the dreary uniform was out of sight and changing into her favourite black skinny jeans and a fluffy pastel-pink jumper. Lessons had dragged on FOREVER today, and her biology teacher had given her a talking-to for her terrible mark in the test last week – she thought everyone had found it hard, but apparently she was bottom of the class. *Whatever!*

The fun and chaotic *Grease* rehearsal at lunch had been the saving grace of her day, although she was starting to panic about the extra lines she needed to learn. She'd joined the production later than the rest of the cast in order to replace Kayleigh (who'd been thrown out, which came as a surprise to literally no one).

'Apparently I need to be "off book" in two weeks, Weenie,' said Abby, picking up the pug again and addressing their reflections in the mirror. 'As in, know all my lines! In TWO WEEKS. Hashtag *help*!' She laughed as the pug stared at her in confusion, then set about tidying her room. She could worry about *Grease* tomorrow.

'I hereby call the first official meeting of Girls Can Vlog . . . to order,' shouted Abby forty minutes later, leaping on the bed and banging her hairbrush against her bookcase.

'Whoa – easy there, chairperson!' giggled Jessie from where she lay stretched out on the carpet, a bowl of sour-cream-and-onion pretzels precariously balanced on her stomach. 'That was loud!'

'Well, I had to stop you lot gassing away somehow!' said Abby, plonking herself back on to the bed with a grin. 'Anyway, now that I've got your attention . . . AHEM! Your ATTENTION . . .'

She stopped talking and glared at Lucy and Hermione, who had discovered Abby's basket of nail polishes and were busy trying out different shades on each other.

'It's OK, Abby, we're l-listening!' said Lucy, as Hermione muttered something about pink not being her colour. 'What's the f-first item on the agenda?'

Ever since they'd decided to switch from Lucy's YouTube channel to a group channel, Abby had basically appointed herself team leader – and they were all happy to let their bubbly, outgoing friend take charge, especially Lucy, who was looking forward to a well-earned break from running a channel on her own. The way she'd battled with her stammer and her confidence issues through vlogging had been a source of inspiration to the whole group.

'First things first: we need to get the rota straight,' said Abby. 'Are we all agreed that between us we'll upload two Girls Can Vlog videos per week?' The point of having a shared channel was that they'd all take turns, vlogging on different days, on a variety of different subjects, alone or in groups, and grow the fanbase together.

'Sounds good to me,' said Jessie, flipping a pretzel high in the air and catching it in her mouth. 'We can brainstorm our ideas for videos at each meeting and decide who's doing what.' The others nodded in agreement.

Abby clapped her hands. 'Awesome. Next up is – our subscribers! How to give them videos they'll LOVE, and how to get our numbers up!'

'Actually, I'm glad you've raised this,' said Hermione, blowing on her nail polish and using her other hand to nudge open the pages of a notebook. 'I've thrown together some statistics, and although we haven't uploaded any content yet, the Girls Can Vlog channel already has fifty-four subscribers. I cross-checked against Lucy's subscriber list and most of them come from her channel.'

'Yeah – a few people left comments below the f-final LucyLocket vlog, saying they would follow us to our new channel right away,' chipped in Lucy. 'N-not as many as

I'd hoped, though. Feels a bit de-depressing going from over a thousand subscribers to fifty-four.'

Jessie jumped to her feet, upturning the bowl and scattering pretzels everywhere – much to Weenie's delight.

'Let's not panic. The key, my friends, is content.' She gestured dramatically to the skies. 'Content, content, content! People only subscribe to a channel once they know what they're getting and wanna see more of it. So we need to send a clear message about Girls Can Vlog delivering *amazing*, *inspirational*, *addictive* videos from our very first vlog.' She emphasized each word with a karate side kick.

'The very vlog that we are recording in a minute! Assuming Jess doesn't take one of us out with her crazy moves,' laughed Abby, edging away from the kicks. 'So let's get thinking. Jess, you've got that Halloween candy left over – food challenges are always fun to include – and we all need to come across as really chatty and friendly.' She glanced at Hermione, who was still flicking through her notebook.

'What, so I'm not always that chatty.' Hermione sighed, looking up from under her fringe and catching Abby's eye. 'But sometimes I think it's best when we just act like ourselves. So what if I'm kind of shy sometimes? Don't we want people to like us for who we are?'

'Hermione's right,' said Lucy. 'We can't all be mega-chatty all the time. Anyway, I think the f-four of us balance each other out really well!'

Abby nodded and flashed an apologetic smile at Hermione. 'Totally. I just meant we should keep our energy up. We *are* great together!'

'Ooh, SPEAKING of being "great together" . . . anything you'd like to share with us, Luce?' said Jessie.

'YES, LUCY,' said Abby meaningfully. Hermione giggled and smiled at Lucy.

Lucy blushed. 'I have n-no idea what you mean.'

'You don't?' Abby looked round at the others, enjoying the moment. 'My mistake, I guess. It's just, I was under the impression you'd been on this, like, super-hot date with the guy you'd fancied, *massively* fancied, for weeks, and it was pretty much the most exciting thing that had happened to you in ages, and yet you failed to update your besties within twenty-four hours?'

'Well, the thing is . . . S-Sam and I . . .' Lucy trailed off awkwardly, occupying herself with patting Weenie.

Jessie looked at her in disbelief. 'You can't leave it there! Sam and I . . . went for a swim? Sam and I . . . ran away to Vegas and got married? Sam and I . . . got abducted by aliens and had our brains switched?'

'Guys!' cried Hermione as Lucy continued to stroke Weenie in silence. 'Leave her alone.' She lowered her voice sensitively. 'Maybe the reason she hasn't told us about it is . . . she just didn't have the perfect time she was expecting?' But she too couldn't help looking curiously at Lucy, who laughed.

'Thanks, H. But actually the date was . . . n-nice. *Really* nice.' The others shrieked and wolf-whistled.

'So why didn't you reply to my texts, you foxy lady!' said Abby.

'I was j-just letting it sink in, I guess . . . Sorry to act mysteriously.' Lucy gazed dreamily into space. 'Anyway, it wasn't r-really that dramatic. We just went for a burger, then a walk, then a coffee, then for another walk. We ch-chatted for hours.' Ignoring the shrieks and giggles, she ploughed on, suddenly unable to stop talking. 'I think I like him . . . I-like him a lot. More than before. Thinking about it, I m-might even be in love!' She blushed and hid her face behind a cushion.

They all squealed with excitement. Abby jumped down from the bed and hugged her. 'Ooh, I'm so pumped for you! Lucy and Sa-am sitting in a tree . . . K-I-S-S– wait, *have* you actually kissed?'

Lucy looked down at Weenie beside her. 'Did me and S-Sam kiss, Weenie? Did we? Y-yes! We kissed. On the walk. By a lake. W-well, more of a pond.'

'Woohoo!' yelled Abby. 'I can't believe I'm only hearing this now.' She addressed the group. 'And this reminds me, guys, I might have my eye on someone too!'

Hermione rolled her eyes. 'Who? Charlie? I hate to

break it to you, Abs, but that's not exactly news.' The others laughed. Charlie was one half of the Prankingstein YouTube channel (Abby's brother, Josh, was the other half) and definitely easy on the eye. He always made Abby go weird and giggly when he was around.

'No! He's just my brother's friend – please! No, I mean Ben – you know the one who's Kenickie in *Grease*? He's got some really good dance moves, and his voice is amazing. I'm pretty sure he winked at me in rehearsal today . . . so, basically, it's only a matter of time until we're double-dating, Luce!' She leaned over to high-five her friend.

'Sounds good!' laughed Lucy. 'Now . . . sorry to break up the gossip session, but m-maybe we should go back to vlog prep?'

'Yeah,' said Hermione, grabbing her notebook and flipping through the pages. 'So where were we? Halloween candy – and please subscribe!'

VLOG 1

Welcome to Our New Channel + Super-Sour Challenge!

7:30

FADE IN: ABBY'S BEDROOM – DAY

ABBY, LUCY, HERMIONE and JESSIE are scrunched together on the end of Abby's bed. Hot-pink fairy lights are strung up around the bedposts; tea lights flicker around the room.

ALL
Hi, guys!

ABBY

It's hard for us to know who's watching, but some of you might remember us from the fantastic Lucy's channel.

They all point at LUCY.

ABBY (CONTINUED)

We did some group videos together, so this channel will give you more of the same!

LUCY

It's n-not that I didn't love having my own channel, but this is way less p-pressure on me – and you'll get to see more of these beautiful girls, so it's all good!

ABBY

Especially as you have a BOYFRIEND now and will probably only have time to do COUPLY things.

LUCY shoves her.

LUCY

I'm still completely committed to v-vlogging AS YOU KNOW.

Plus I'm n-not the only one with a LOVE INTEREST.

ABBY tackles her to the ground before she can say any more.

HERMIONE

Now, now, children!

JESSIE

Can we PLEASE do the super-sour challenge?

HERMIONE looks at her notebook.

HERMIONE

Not yet! We have to welcome our lovely subscribers properly –
looks straight into camera – SORRY, VIEWERS. Some of us
seem to be behaving like five-year-olds today! The point of this
vlog was to say thanks for checking us out, guys! I, er, hope
you'll stick with us despite this chaotic start . . .

ABBY gathers herself and neatens her hair.

ABBY

Yeah, it was just to give everyone a taste of our videos and to
encourage you to tune in twice a week. And to ask for your
feedback about the kind of videos you want to see. We're
still working out how regular our content will be, but we will
definitely upload a new vlog at least twice a week
and we can cover loads of
things . . .

ABBY starts ticking them off on
her fingers as she says them.

ABBY (CONTINUED)

. . . make-up, fashion, shopping hauls, baking, fitness, tag videos, all kinds of challenges, pranks, pizza parties, yoga challenges, dance routines, room tours, makeovers, ooh, I know! How to make sushi—

JESSIE

(interrupts)

– AND super-sour challenges!

All laugh. HERMIONE takes notes frantically, then throws her pen on the floor in relief.

ABBY

OK, OK! Point taken. We'll get started, then . . . over to you, Jess!

JESSIE dishes out the super-sour eyeball gobstoppers and puts the bag on the bed.

JESSIE

So I ordered these specially from the US for Halloween, but still haven't tried them – apparently they start out sweet and then get more and more sour. The challenge is to see who can keep them in their mouth the longest! Ready? Here goes!

JESSIE pops hers in her mouth and the others follow suit. They smile and exchange looks before slowly their faces drop. HERMIONE looks particularly horrified, wincing more and more as the seconds tick by.

HERMIONE stands and runs to the bin off camera, spitting her gobstopper out.

HERMIONE

OH MY GOD, that was so disgusting!

ABBY paces around the room, shaking her head. LUCY has her hand over her mouth. JESSIE is sitting calmly with a smile on her face.

HERMIONE (CONTINUED)

Guys, how are you *doing* that?

ABBY and LUCY look at each other, then run and spit theirs out. JESSIE shrugs then crunches her gobstopper to pieces and swallows it.

JESSIE

Too easy! All I ask for is a little bit of competition from you guys in these eating challenges!

HERMIONE

How did you do it? I nearly vommed!

ABBY

(still grimacing)

So . . . not sure if that's what you wanted to see today,

viewers, but there you have it! Three sets of very unhappy taste buds and one example of Jess's superhuman powers. If you liked it, give us a thumbs-up down below and leave a com—
NO! WEENIE!

WEENIE has found the gobstoppers on the bed and is sniffing them curiously, then gives one a lick. WEENIE yelps in dismay before running from the room. All gasp.

ABBY

Oh dear – I should go and see if he's OK . . . Er, bye, everyone!

All wave.

FADE OUT.

Views: 156 and counting

Subscribers: 103

Comments:

billythekid: Haha, poor Weenie!

PrankingsteinJosh: Stop trying to poison our dog, sis!

Amazing_Abby_xxx: He's fine . . . Happily eating some *actual* dog food right now . . .

queen_dakota: Ugh you guys are back – oops, I forgot to subscribe! #sorrynotsorry

MagicMorgan: Yay Girls Can Vlog! Can't wait to collab some time x

StephSaysHi: So excited 🙂 Welcome back, ladies – I'd love to see more beauty videos ♥♥

pinksparkles: And more hauls! *subscribes*

(scroll down to see 5 more comments)

Chapter Two

'Ouch, my foot! No, Abby, it's this way!'

A flustered Abby grinned apologetically at her dance partner, Eric, as he dragged her in the right direction. Luckily she'd known him for ages and he was a patient, understanding kind of guy – the kind of guy who didn't mind having his toes repeatedly squashed, apparently. Well, not too much. He had the role of Roger in *Grease*, playing Abby's (Jan's) date at the high-school dance, and today they were rehearsing the hand-jive dance scene. It was quick and energetic and, however hard Abby tried, she just couldn't keep up.

'OK, I think we're all ready for a break, team.' As Ms

Kusama, the Head of Drama, went to switch off the music, Abby sighed with relief. She picked up her script to make a few notes then walked over to Ben, who was grinning at her from the other side of the studio.

'What are you laughing at?' said Abby, pulling out her ponytail and shaking her long blonde hair free.

Ben pulled a mock-serious face. 'Nothing. Definitely not your hilarious inability to pick up those dance moves – it's kind of painful to watch. Poor Eric – first Kayleigh as his partner and now you!'

'Excuse me, Benjamin!' said Abby playfully. 'Remember I've only just joined, will you? And please never compare me to Kayleigh again. Literally nobody deserves that.'

Ben chuckled. 'I wasn't comparing you – though now you come to mention it, you do have similar hair, and eyes, and, you know, your personality isn't THAT dissimilar . . . JUST KIDDING!' he added as Abby's face darkened with horror. She whacked him with her script.

'Ow!' he cried in an exaggerated, high-pitched voice, and they both burst out laughing.

'I don't know what's so funny, but I'm fed up with your unprofessionalism spoiling our rehearsals, Abby,' said Dakota, coming over to them, reeking strongly of vanilla as usual and shadowed by one of her ever-present friends, the mostly-silent Ameeka. 'Ms Kusama's shown you that routine, like, four times now. What is wrong with you?'

'Don't worry, Dakota – I'll get it!' said Abby. 'And it's not for you to worry about anyway – that's Ms Kusama's job.' *Why does that girl have to be such a massive pain?* she thought as Ben sloped off to the drinks machine. Dakota had the role of sassy Rizzo, but any time she wasn't in a scene she acted like she was the director and producer too.

'I hope you realize this is a serious production,' continued Dakota snidely.

'*Really* serious,' drawled Ameeka, examining her nails. 'People are, like, paying money to come.'

'Exactly,' said Dakota, lowering her voice as Ms Kusama walked past. 'Are you sure you're up to it, Abby?' she hissed. 'I mean, it's not some dumb after-school drama club – we're expected to pull our weight and practise at home too.'

'Got it. Thanks, Dakota!' said Abby, moving away. *Ugh, what an annoying busybody!* She caught Ben's eye and mimed putting a gun to her head. He laughed, which made her heart skip. It had been so much fun talking to him before they'd been so rudely interrupted. They had chatted in class before, but recently things felt different and, even though Abby was probably getting ahead of herself by bragging to the girls about him, she was pretty sure that he was flirting with her, that he'd *noticed* her. She'd definitely noticed him – how on earth had she failed to register his dark good looks before now? His eyelashes were longer than hers, for goodness sake!

Abby cleared her throat nervously as the teacher called her and Eric to try the routine one more time. Ben leaned against the wall and watched, sipping on his can of Fanta. The choreography was really difficult and how on earth was she meant to concentrate on the dance steps while he was gazing at her with an amused look on his face? Her stomach was doing flip-flops. Abby fumbled her way through the routine, also trying to block out Dakota and Ameeka's evil glares.

At least when I'm vlogging I don't have anyone staring back at me, she thought as she messed up yet again.

'Miss, I don't think she's getting it,' called Dakota, her face the picture of helpfulness. 'I picked it up really quickly so maybe I can stay after school to show her, one to one? I'm happy to do it!'

Abby raised her eyebrows. She knew that Dakota enjoyed pointing out other people's mistakes, thrived on it in fact, but Abby was surprised that she would offer to give up her time to help her. Maybe she was just trying to suck up to the teacher.

If so, it worked. 'Dakota, that's really kind of you,' said Ms Kusama gratefully. 'I'm sure that with your help Abby will pick up the routine in no time. She just needs a bit more practice. Does that work for you, Abby?' Abby nodded dumbly, not knowing what else to do. 'Great!' The teacher beamed. 'Now, gang – time

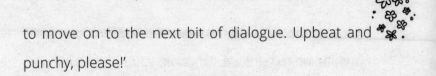

to move on to the next bit of dialogue. Upbeat and punchy, please!'

Later, Abby begged Eric to come too so that she wouldn't have to face Dakota alone, but he had football practice.

'It'll be better for you to nail the routine on your own,' he said, getting his boots out of his locker. 'Then we can blow them away together at our next rehearsal.'

'OK, thanks anyway!' she called as she dashed to the studio where she'd arranged to meet Dakota. Despite finding her enormously annoying, Abby was slightly scared of the most popular girl in their year and didn't want to keep her waiting. Arriving, she opened the door and saw Dakota sitting on the piano bench, her long legs elegantly crossed as she tapped a message into her phone.

'Hi,' said Abby tentatively. It was the first time she'd ever been alone in a room with Dakota, she realized. 'Erm, thanks for doing this, I guess. I'm hoping we can get it over with quite quickly.'

Dakota looked up and smoothed her long, glossy

hair over one shoulder, a beautiful but mocking smile creeping on to her face. 'Oh, wait, you didn't think I was actually going to coach you, did you?'

'Er, yes?' said Abby, baffled. 'Isn't that what we agreed?'

Dakota sniggered scornfully. 'This is awkward.' She held up her phone, pouted and snapped a selfie before continuing. 'Look, let me spell things out for you . . . *Obviously* I don't have time to hold your hand and teach you an *incredibly* basic dance, you can sort that out yourself, one would hope! I know, why don't you make a stupid vlog about it?'

'A vlo– huh?' Abby snapped out of her daze. 'What exactly is your problem, Dakota? I know you're jealous of our channel, but why did you drag me down here if you didn't want to help with the routine?'

'Jealous of your – oh please!' Dakota yawned, as if she couldn't be bothered with the rest of the sentence. 'No, I've just come to give you a message. Keep away from Ben. I saw your lame attempts at flirting earlier, and so before you embarrass yourself any further I'm letting you know he's off limits.' She held up her phone for another selfie. 'Not that you could get him anyway,' she murmured through her pressed-together lips.

'Off limits?' Abby was dumbstruck. 'Are you guys . . . uh . . . *together*?'

Dakota finished her selfie and stood, picking up her school bag. 'Don't worry about the details – you should save your tiny amount of brainpower for learning the dance routine. You got the message about Ben – that's all there is to it. Later, loser.'

And with that she was gone. For a few seconds Abby just stood there, baffled and seething with anger at the same time, furious tears welling in her eyes.

15.45

Abby: Just been warned off Ben good and proper – by Dakota!! I mean, are they even together? 😠

15.46

Lucy: NO?! WHAT PLANET IS SHE ON??

Lucy's reply made her feel slightly better, but Abby was shaken and intimidated. She was also annoyed at herself for allowing Dakota to get to her. On top of which, she now had to go home and try to learn the hand-jive steps herself – as well as doing her homework *and* filming and editing her first solo video for the channel.

Abby was really excited about her vlog, but wished she'd had more time to prepare. She wanted it to be so perfect. There was no stalling, though. She'd promised the girls she'd upload it tonight and she knew it was really important to keep the viewers interested with new content. It was a make-up tutorial, but she'd have to calm down a bit before pressing 'record', she thought, catching sight of her red-cheeked, dishevelled face in the giant studio mirror. Oh great – she had a massive spot on her chin. Ben would have been staring right at it when they were chatting earlier. She wanted to crawl into a hole and die!

VLOG 2

Amazing Abby's Natural
Make-up Tutorial 7:10

FADE IN: ABBY'S BEDROOM

ABBY sitting on her bed, wearing a purple jumper with pompoms and jeans, hair pushed back from her face with a black hairband. WEENIE is curled up next to her.

ABBY

Hi, everybody! I am so excited to be the first one to post a solo video on this channel and really hope that you all love it and that I don't let everyone down! Phew! Pressure! I'm going to try really hard not to ramble too much – everyone tells me I do – and get right down to business as there's loads of stuff I want to cover.

(*takes a deep breath and smiles*)

So let's get started. Lots of my friends have asked me to show them a simple everyday make-up routine, which you can wear *even* if you aren't allowed to wear make-up by your parents or school. My school is pretty strict about this . . .

ABBY makes a silly grimace.

ABBY (CONTINUED)

But today I am having a spot crisis . . . a ZIT DISASTER, in fact . . . which unfortunately isn't that unusual. Whether it's too much chocolate or greasy food – which my mum is always warning me not to eat – or just hormones, spots can really get you down and knock your self-confidence. But don't let them ruin your life! Here's how to fight back.

JOSH bursts into the room. He picks up the camera and starts filming ABBY close up.

JOSH

Yuck! Look at your face! You've got the bubonic plague! What is this?
(picks up a make-up bottle)
Concealer, yeah you need it!

ABBY jumps up, grabbing the bottle.

ABBY

Get out! Get out! You're ruining my video.

ABBY pushes JOSH towards the door, grabbing the camera.

JOSH

OK, OK! If the concealer doesn't work, maybe use a bin bag

to cover your entire head? Haha, love you really, sis! Promise

you'll do a vlog with us soon?

ABBY

Whatever, Josh!

ABBY slams the door, giggling.

ABBY (CONTINUED)

Sorry about that! Ugh, brothers! So

anyway . . . here's my vanity table. I got

this for my last birthday and I completely

love it. The mirror and the lights are really

flattering, and there's room for all my

make-up. Sorry it's a bit of a mess – I

didn't have time to tidy. Ew, don't know what that's doing here!

ABBY removes a doggy chew stick from vanity table.

ABBY (CONTINUED)

Weenie, were you up here? Naughty boy! I'll put my camera

here so you can see my face . . .

ABBY positions camera on tripod.

ABBY (CONTINUED)

OK, let's go. First of all, you need to have a good cleansing

routine both in the morning and at night. I put my hair back

out of my face with this hairband then wash with a foaming

product and water, which I've already done. After cleansing, I

put on moisturizer – which is really important. I'm just using

cheap drugstore products because that's all I can afford, but

they work as well as the expensive brands as long as you apply

them properly. I don't use a heavy foundation because it's not

allowed at school and anyway my mum would kill me! Instead I use a BB cream or a tinted moisturizer and apply it with my fingers.

(applies cream)

Next you need a matt concealer and it's really important to choose the right colour for your skin tone, not too light or dark as that just draws attention to the spots. Take a tiny brush and apply the concealer to the centre of the spot – not too much! – and allow it to settle into the skin. Then dab on a little bit of powder and dust over the area.

(demonstrates this)

You could also apply the concealer under your eyes to cover up dark circles or on any redness. Next set the concealer with a light translucent powder to help it last all day. See? The spot is almost invisible! Result! Then I like to use a little bit of blusher on my cheeks just to give myself

a healthy colour. Finish off with
a slick of mascara and finally
some clear lip gloss.

ABBY pouts and flutters her eyelashes.

ABBY (CONTINUED)

So that's it for the 'no make-up' make-up routine! When you
are going out, you can add eyeshadow and eyeliner, more
mascara and finally some coloured lip gloss or lipstick. I hope
this tutorial was helpful; let me know with a thumbs-up below!
Another time I'll show you how to put on some smoky eye
make-up, perfect for a party in the autumn or winter! Byee!
See you soon!

ABBY picks up WEENIE and they both wave goodbye.

FADE OUT.

Views: 276 and counting

Subscribers: 179

Comments:

RedVelvet: Wow! Really professional tutorial. Way to go, girl!

★ ★ ★

pink_sprinkles: ↑↑ @Amazing_Abby RedVelvet watched and commented! Goals!

queen_dakota: Mount Vesuvius comes to mind! Suggest burka . . .

LucyLocket: Yay! Fabby Abby looking hot! ❤

ShyGirl1: My mum won't let me wear make-up yet . . . ☹

funnyinternetperson54: Josh is right, you HAVE to do a collab with Prankingstein!! ☺

MagicMorgan: Agree!!

(scroll down to see 35 more comments)

⏩

Chapter Three

'And here's my line of make-up brushes, available in shops up and down the country! They've got the *Amazing Abby* rosebud branding on the side, as you can see, and they're specially designed to ensure your make-up looks supermodel *flawless* . . .'

The camera zoomed closer and closer as Abby demonstrated, using her new blusher brush to spread a shimmer of gold dust across her cheekbones, creating the trademark bronzed-goddess look that her viewers loved . . . adding more and more and more . . .

Abby woke with a start, her hand stroking the side of her own face. Wow – that had been the best dream ever, not that she'd be telling anyone about it – cringe! She lay on the pillow and grinned, reliving the glory of it all.

As a renowned beauty expert with millions of subscribers, she'd been asked to develop a whole range of products. She was the most popular vlogger in the world, living a life of luxury, and at one point she'd been on a private tropical island talking into her limited edition Amazing Abby iPhone and eating expensive sushi on a sunlounger, in her favourite designer bikini, while her gorgeous pop-star boyfriend massaged her feet . : .

If only! she thought, finally hauling herself up and staring at her bed head in the mirror. Her subconscious must have got carried away after all the nice comments on her make-up tutorial yesterday, and glancing at the Girls Can Vlog channel on her phone she let out another squeak of joy at the number of views, which had risen overnight. Her first solo vlog had been a hit! Well – not by RedVelvet standards, but still. Maybe if she put a load of work into her tutorials, her dream could one day become a reality . . . Maybe?

Later, she daydreamed through the first class at school, English, doodling some Amazing Abby logo ideas on the margin of her exercise book, only coming back to earth as the teacher, Miss Piercy, announced that she was handing back their latest essays.

The assignment had been to compare two of Shakespeare's sonnets and Abby had sort of rushed through her essay without rereading it before handing it in. But hopefully it hadn't been as bad as she'd thought. Abby watched nervously as Miss Piercy circulated the room, returning the essays and singling out the occasional pupil for praise – 'impressive, Ameeka' – ugh! Abby turned away as Ameeka raised a smug eyebrow.

'Abby, see me after class, would you, please?' said Miss Piercy, dropping the essay on her desk.

Abby's heart sank and she heard Kayleigh and Dakota giggling behind her. Her essay was covered with Miss Piercy's bright orange scrawl and, flipping the paper over, she gasped when she saw it: a big fat F, her first ever!

'We'll talk about it,' whispered Miss Piercy, putting a hand on her shoulder. 'Don't worry.'

Hermione, a few seats along, shot Abby a questioning look. Abby shrugged, attempting a smile despite the hot tears of shame that were welling in her eyes, and nudged her essay under her notebook so that nobody would see the awful grade. Her essay hadn't been *that* bad, had it?

The rest of the lesson went by in a blur, and before she knew it she was at Miss Piercy's desk, trying to explain herself. 'It's just . . . I'm really busy with *Grease* and stuff . . . Sorry, Miss Piercy! I'll try harder next time, I promise.'

'You do seem to have a lot on, Abby,' said Miss Piercy, 'but I don't know if that's the only problem here. This is very sloppy work indeed. Most of the sentences barely made sense, and it wasn't even clear whether you'd read the sonnets.'

Abby blushed. 'I-I did read them, but . . . they didn't really stay with me, you know?'

'I see,' said Miss Piercy, although the look she gave

Abby suggested that she didn't see at all. 'Perhaps you could have spent a bit longer reading the poems and thinking about the symbolism of the language. We need to give Shakespeare our proper attention if we want to get to the nitty-gritty of what he's trying to express.'

Yeah, nitty-gritty, sure, thought Abby, starting to feel a bit bored. She'd be late for her next lesson, and she wanted to check on her zit; she was seeing Ben in a couple of hours at lunchtime rehearsal. 'I'll totally work harder on the next one, Miss Piercy, I promise.'

'Actually, Abby, I'd like you to redo this one, if you wouldn't mind,' said Miss Piercy gently. 'GCSEs are coming up very soon and I'd like to help you master the art of a well-crafted essay. Could you read my suggestions and have another bash by next week?' She always phrased things as if she were asking her pupils a favour, but Abby knew there was no getting away from this – it was an order. She grinned weakly.

'Okey-dokey, I'll have Take Two with you on Monday. Thanks, miss!' she said. 'Gotta dash!' She smiled brightly at her teacher, who gazed at Abby thoughtfully for a moment before excusing her.

'What was THAT all about?' asked Hermione, who had hung around to wait for her outside the classroom.

Abby shoved the essay into her bag. 'Nothing much – you know Miss Piercy likes to chat!'

'About what, though?' asked Hermione. 'Was it the essay?'

Abby started walking briskly along the corridor, taking out a hand mirror as she went. 'Come on, H – does it matter? Come and help me sort out this spot – I need concealer, AGAIN! How am I meant to make it as a mega-rich beauty guru if my face isn't completely flawless at all times?'

Zit sorted, Abby buried the terrible grade at the back of her mind for the rest of the morning, finding relief in the *Grease* rehearsal where she finally mastered the hand-jive moves.

'ABOUT TIME,' drawled Ameeka the first time Abby made it all the way through without a mistake.

'She's j-just annoyed she and Dakota can't criticize you any more!' giggled Lucy who was also having a good rehearsal, without too much stammering. 'W-well done, Abs! We're nailing this, you and me!'

The rehearsal was made extra brilliant by the fact that Dakota was distracted today. She'd started worshipping Maxine, who was playing the role of Sandy and was in the year above. Dakota thought she had finally met someone worthy of her attention and had taken to following the older girl around, offering to hold her script and fetch snacks for her at the drop of a hat.

'Quite funny, r-really,' observed Lucy as Maxine smiled impatiently at Dakota before accepting some crisps then turning her back on her. 'It almost makes you feel s-sorry for her. Almost.'

'Great job, everyone,' said Ms Kusama once the hour was up. 'And thank you for giving up your lunch breaks once again. I'm really pleased with the way everything is coming together, and as a reward I'm treating you to Pizza Planet after school. Everyone welcome, free slices on me!'

'YESSS! I love that place!' said Abby, more loudly than she'd planned, raising a laugh from most of the cast.

Their teacher smiled. 'I'm glad my plan meets with your approval, Miss Pinkerton. Oh, and don't forget to text or call your parents for permission first.'

'See you there, Abs,' said Ben, walking past Abby and Lucy as the group dispersed.

Lucy stared after him. 'OMG, Abs – he d-does like you! That comment was one hundred per cent directed at you. I'd be feeling quite offended, actually, if I wasn't s-such a generous and amazing friend. Hey, B-Ben, I like pizza too!' she called after him jokingly.

'Stop it!' said Abby, laughing. 'You already have a boyfriend! Free pizza, though . . . I always said Ms Kusama was an absolute legend.'

The *Grease* cast gathered around two large tables at Pizza Planet. Maxine hadn't joined them and, with nobody around to worship, Dakota was back to her usual tricks. Abby noticed that she'd rolled up her school skirt shorter than ever and added some hoop earrings and an extra coat of thick black mascara.

'Guys, sit here,' Dakota ordered, patting the bench beside her the second that Ben and Eric entered the pizza parlour. Abby rolled her eyes at Lucy. She still wasn't sure whether Dakota actually fancied Ben or just liked to have his attention, as she did with most of the boys in their class.

'That's cool, there's more space here,' said Ben, gesturing to Abby and Lucy's table. 'Thanks anyway, Dakota.'

Abby gasped, then quickly tried to act as if she hadn't noticed. She continued to study the menu and started talking loudly to Lucy about what toppings to order. It was only when Ben sat opposite her and kicked her leg under the table that she allowed herself to look up and meet his eyes, warmly mocking her as usual.

'Oh, um, hey, Ben,' she said. 'How are you?'

'Seriously starving. I've had pizza on my brain all afternoon. What are you having?' He smiled, watching her. 'You seem to be studying your options very thoroughly there.'

Abby lowered the menu. 'Well, you know, it's a big decision – I don't want to rush it. Comet Cheese Feast or Meaty Meteor Madness? It's a tough one.'

He nodded. 'I know, right – cheese or meat. Cheese or meat. The eternal dilemma . . . maybe we could share a half and half?'

Abby glanced at Lucy, with whom she had been planning to share. 'I might g-go for a veggie one – you two carry on,' said Lucy, tactfully starting up a conversation with Eric who was trying to balance a straw on his upper lip.

'OK, you're on,' Abby told Ben. 'Though I don't like the spicy meatballs so you'll have to pick those off my slices.' She ignored the pointed looks of Dakota and Ameeka from the other table. In what world was it illegal to share a pizza? But secretly she felt triumphant. Ben had chosen her over Dakota!

Once everyone had got their food, Dakota and Ameeka started messing around with Ameeka's new selfie stick that she had got for her birthday, taking pictures of their food and squeezing together to pose.

'Careful, girls, you don't want to end up with pizza all over your phone,' warned Ms Kusama, looking over at their table.

'Yes, miss,' they trilled, taking a few final snaps.

'You know what . . . I could murder a double-choc caramel milkshake,' said Ben, his mouth full of pizza.

Abby grimaced. 'That is SO wrong!'

'What? I'm a growing boy!' said Ben, earning a laugh from Eric.

'Er, if you say so!' said Abby, slightly flustered. She tried to match his relaxed tone. 'I can run up and grab you a milkshake if you want? I need to get some napkins anyway.'

She got up from her seat and went over to the counter. This talking-to-boys stuff was harder than she'd thought, but as long as she kept her cool she might be in with a chance . . . Maybe Ben would ask her on a date?

Coming back with the deliciously foaming milkshake, she had to walk past Dakota's table, but she kept her head held high. The girls weren't glaring at her for once so maybe they had got bored of punishing her? Until – OH NO! – suddenly she tripped over something and she was falling. Everything went into slow motion as she watched the milkshake fall out of her hand, the glass crash on the floor, the brown liquid splatter everywhere and Dakota hastily move her foot back where it had been . . .

Before Abby knew it, she was lying on the floor with a grazed knee and palm, covered in chocolate goop, her heart racing frantically. There was a gasp and she heard Lucy cry, 'Oh my god!' from their table.

Then the waves of laughter started. 'Have a nice hashtag *trip*?' cackled a voice that could only be Dakota's, as Abby eased herself up into a sitting position.

'Don't forget to send a postcard,' purred Ameeka, looking down at her.

'Abby, are y-you OK?' Lucy knelt down beside her. 'You tripped – I-look, it was their stupid selfie stick.' She pointed under the table.

'Well, it's not our fault if she can't look where she's going,' smirked Dakota, chewing delicately on the straw of her Diet Coke. 'Too busy bringing milkshakes to her lover boy.'

Taking Lucy's hand and getting to her feet, Abby looked down and saw the selfie stick jutting out from under the table. The phone had been removed from it and the stick was sticking out suspiciously far.

'You kicked that there on purpose!' she exclaimed.

'Oh please,' drawled Ameeka, confirming Abby's suspicions by hastily removing the stick as Ms Kusama hurried over, pizza slice still in hand.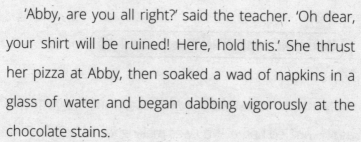

'Abby, are you all right?' said the teacher. 'Oh dear, your shirt will be ruined! Here, hold this.' She thrust her pizza at Abby, then soaked a wad of napkins in a glass of water and began dabbing vigorously at the chocolate stains.

'Awkward – her shirt is going see-through!' announced Dakota at the top of her voice.

Abby cringed and remembered that she was wearing her grossest, greyest sports bra today. She couldn't bear to look at Ben.

'I think it's fine, thanks, miss,' she said shakily, handing back the pizza. 'But I might get going now . . .' She couldn't wait to be out of there.

'Are you sure?' asked Ms Kusama.

'I'll g-go with her,' offered Lucy.

'It's fine,' said Abby, grabbing her stuff and throwing her coat over her wet shirt. Her knee was killing her and she just wanted to be alone. 'It's a short walk home for me – I'll see you guys tomorrow.'

18.35

> **Unknown number:** Hey there, pizza pal!

Abby glanced at the phone which pinged in her pocket just as she arrived home. Who was making fun of her now?

18.36

Abby: Who is this?

18.38

Unknown number: Ben.
Lucy gave me ur number –
I wanted to check u were OK?

18.39

Abby: Yeah fine. Not my most graceful moment 🙂

18.40

Ben: Cool. Still waiting for my milkshake btw 😜

18.40

Abby: NOT HAPPENING!!

18.41

Ben: Joking. See you on Monday xx

Two kisses! *Take* that, *Dakota*, Abby thought with a grin. Spirits soaring, despite her embarrassing splat earlier, she started to prepare for her next vlog, which she'd be shooting tomorrow. Hooray for the weekend!

VLOG 3

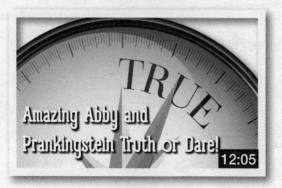

Amazing Abby and
Prankingstein Truth or Dare!

12:05

FADE IN: ABBY'S FAMILY ROOM – DAY

ABBY, JOSH and CHARLIE are sitting on the sofa. There are two bowls with folded slips of paper on the coffee table.

ABBY

Hey there, viewers! Hope you enjoyed Lucy and Hermione's amazing book-haul video the other day – link down below – now for something a bit more raucous. Today I'm doing a collab with these two guys – better known as Prankingstein –

aka Josh and Charlie! Aka my brother and his mate!

JOSH and CHARLIE wave.

ABBY (CONTINUED)

We're going to do the ultimate truth or dare because you guys

have been asking for one. It should be really fun!

JOSH

So it's the usual drill where we pick either from the truth or

dare bowls and have to do what the paper says. The challenges

come partly from your suggestions and partly from us. First up

is Charlie. Truth or dare?

CHARLIE

Dare. *(He picks one from the bowl)*

Oh man! I don't believe it . . .

(reads out)

Eat a tablespoon of Weenie's dog food.

ABBY

(laughs)

Yes! That's hilarious. Allow me to serve you . . .

Edited as high-speed footage, ABBY picks up the camera and goes to the kitchen, where we see her collect WEENIE's food bowl and get a spoon from the drawer. She returns to the family room, and hands a spoonful of dog food to CHARLIE.

ABBY (CONTINUED)

Here you go – *bon appetit*!

CHARLIE grimaces and puts a spoonful in his mouth. He pauses before swallowing.

CHARLIE

(retching)

Yuck! No!

CHARLIE opens a box of breath
mints and tips them into his mouth.

CHARLIE (CONTINUED)

That was disgusting. Weenie, how can you put up

with that, mate?

WEENIE runs around and barks off camera.

CHARLIE (CONTINUED)

It tastes worse than my grandmother's corned-beef hash! Abby,

your turn now. Truth or dare?

ABBY

Truth. Help, I'm really nervous about this. *(Picks a paper from the other bowl)* OMG! I can't answer that . . .

CHARLIE

No excuses – I just ate dog food!

ABBY

Fine.

(slowly reads out)

Who was your first kiss?

JOSH bursts out laughing and makes loud kissing noises. ABBY covers her face with her hand.

ABBY (CONTINUED)

Well, if I have to . . . it was – oh this is sooo embarrassing – this guy I met on holiday in Spain last summer.

JOSH

You mean that little creep *Juan*? So
that's what you were doing on the
beach! I should have told Mum!

ABBY

Well, you were off with that French girl anyway!

(blushes)

It was perfectly innocent.

CHARLIE

(meaningfully)

But did you enjoy it?

ABBY

I don't know! That wasn't part of the question. Your turn now, Josh!

JOSH

OK. Dare.

(reads out)

Stick your bare foot in the toilet and then suck your toe!

Gross! Who thought of that?

CHARLIE

I think you did, buddy! Go on, then, we're waiting . . .

ABBY bounces on the sofa, shrieking with excitement.

ABBY

Yes, go ahead, bro!

CHARLIE

We'll just follow you with the camera to the loo to make sure
you really do this!

Edited as high-speed footage, the camera follows JOSH upstairs to the bathroom.

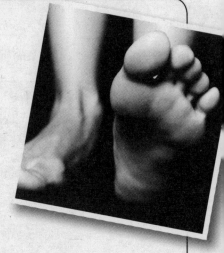

JOSH makes a face as he takes off his sock and dips his toes into the toilet bowl.

ABBY

Eeew! This is so wrong.

Followed by the camera, JOSH hops back downstairs to the sofa and sits down with ABBY and CHARLIE.

CHARLIE

Come on now . . . Don't be shy . . . Let's see you do it!

JOSH wriggles about and lifts his big toe up to his mouth. He grins at the camera before he pops it in for a second.

JOSH

Yum, yum, yum! What's for dessert?

ABBY

So vile! No one will ever snog you again after seeing that! OK,

Charlie, you next. Truth or dare?

CHARLIE

Truth.

(picks a slip of paper, reads)

What's the most embarrassing thing that's ever happened to you?

Hmmm. Let me think.

JOSH

Dude, your whole life is an embarrassment!

ABBY

(whacks Josh)

Don't be mean!

CHARLIE

I've got it. When I was in Year Five, I had a crush on this girl and I'd finally got up the courage to ask her to be my partner for a role-playing thing in drama class. I came up to her and somehow the words that came out of my mouth were, 'Hey, Mum!'

ABBY and JOSH laugh at him.

CHARLIE (CONTINUED)
It still makes me cringe and I have no idea why I said it.

JOSH

I remember that! Everybody laughed.

ABBY

OMG! How sweet! Poor little Charlie.

CHARLIE pretends to strangle ABBY and they both start wrestling on the sofa.

JOSH

Er, guys . . . get a room?

ABBY

What? Shut up! OK, my turn and this might have to be the last
one as we're running out of time . . . This time I'm going to be
brave and choose a dare!

(picks from the bowl and reads)

Kiss someone in the room on the lips for ten seconds. No way!

JOSH

Haha! That must be a viewer's suggestion.

ABBY

(to Josh)

Well, I obviously can't kiss you as you're my brother . . .
and you've stuck your pooey toe in your mouth! I'd probably
die from the germs you've got. So I haven't really got much
choice . . . This is sooo embarrassing . . .

JOSH

I'm sure Charlie won't mind.

CHARLIE

Anything for the viewers . . . When you're ready, Abby!

ABBY

(to camera)

Brainwave! OK, I'm ready. Here goes.

ABBY snatches WEENIE up and gives him a great big smooch on the lips.

JOSH

That's cheating!

CHARLIE looks stunned then bursts out laughing.

CHARLIE

Well played, Abby!

ABBY

No offence, Charlie. Maybe another time . . . if you're VERY lucky. Anyway, that's all for now. Give us a thumbs-up below if you liked the video and if you'd like to see more truth or dares give me your suggestions down below. And you can catch Josh and Charlie on the Prankingstein Channel too. By-eee!

ABBY, JOSH and CHARLIE wave.

FADE OUT.

Views: 343 and counting

Subscribers: 273

Comments:

MagicMorgan: Really shipping this Charlie and Abby thing!

JazzieJessie: #CHABBY ♥♥♥

StephSaysHi: Funny!! Felt so ill when Josh sucked his toe!

girlscanvlogfan: Loving every single video so far 👍

xxrainbowxx: Haha, CHABBY ftw!

StalkerGurl: Josh – marry me xxx

queen_dakota: Lame. Too bad you didn't end up in the toilet @Amazing_Abby_xxx! That would have been a laugh.

(scroll down to see 87 more comments)

Chapter Four

'Abs, are you getting a lift with us?' shouted Josh on Monday morning.

Abby looked up from rewatching their truth-or-dare vlog with Charlie. It had been so much fun and she had to admit Charlie was looking pretty cute these days. Plus he'd definitely been up for that snog! Had it been just for the dare, though, or *did* he maybe fancy her?

She gazed at the screen, wondering what he thought of all the teasing comments that had been posted about them as a couple. *Chabby, ha ha ha!* she'd texted Jessie. You had to give it to her – the girl was hilarious.

'ABBY!' yelled Josh. 'Last chance!'

'Don't worry, I'll walk!' she shouted back. 'Just finishing my English essay.' She tore herself away from her laptop and glanced down at her desk at the supposedly new and improved essay for Miss Piercy. She had spent an hour on it yesterday, but she had a gut feeling it still wasn't that great – maybe she could work on it a little more at lunchtime. Her phone beeped.

8.12

Ben: Good weekend? So not ready for biology test today! x

Abby nearly dropped the phone, a thousand different thoughts hitting her in quick succession.

Ben texted me – again! He must really like me!

Then: *BIOLOGY TEST – nooooo! I completely forgot!*

Then: *Wait – who do I like more? Ben – or Charlie? Ben is maybe more my type, but Charlie is just so cute and funny!*

Then: *OMG, I am going to be so late for school! But first I should text Ben back so it's not awkward when I see him!*

Then: *Argh – where is my biology textbook?*

8.14

> **Abby:** 100% not ready either. Save me! x

Despite his message, Ben seemed to be doing fine, she noticed in the biology lab a couple of hours later. Hunched over his paper, he looked completely absorbed, methodically filling in the answers. Abby continued to stare at his white-shirted back, then glanced at Hermione, similarly immersed beside her, then out of the window, then back at her paper. It was a multiple choice quiz, at least, so she could make random guesses, but she was shocked by how out of her depth she felt – bewildered by each and every question.

Q. When a root bends in the direction of the force of gravity:

a) the top side grows more than the bottom side

b) the bottom side grows more than the top side

c) the top and bottom sides grow at the same rate

What did it even mean? Abby had the faintest recollection of a diagram of plant roots the teacher had once drawn, but nothing more. Sometimes she found it really hard to absorb information in class.

Her pen hovered over the answers, and she kicked herself – why hadn't she revised? Mum had been upset when Abby had told her about her English essay, and now she was probably going to get in hot water over this too.

She looked up as Hermione hummed contentedly, turning over the paper. *She makes it look so easy*, Abby thought. Then she noticed that they were on the same page of the exam – and that she could see Hermione's answers. Before she realized what she was doing, she started ticking all the boxes that Hermione had ticked. At least she would get *some* answers right.

'That was horrendous!' said Ben, coming up to her in the canteen at break. 'Who in their right mind would come up with the idea of quizzing us on a Monday morning?'

Abby pulled a face. 'Can we please not talk about it?'

'That bad, eh?' he said sympathetically. 'OK, subject change . . . I see you're drinking a water. No more milkshakes for you after Friday?'

'Ben! Can we please not talk about that either!' she giggled. 'And anyway, I was getting it for you, remember? You're the whole reason I had to spend Friday night soaking my shirt.'

He raised his eyebrows. 'Sounds hot.'

Abby blushed. 'ANYWAY I am so not over being annoyed with Dakota.' She'd been mulling it over all weekend and the more she thought about it the more convinced she was that it had been a set-up.

'She didn't mean it,' said Ben. 'I'm sure the selfie-stick thing was a genuine mistake.' Abby gave him a look. 'No, seriously. She can actually be quite nice – we've been practising the Rizzo and Kenickie stuff and she's kind of funny once you get to know her.'

Abby's heart sank, and she tried not to let her dismay show on her face. She knew that Ben and Dakota's characters in *Grease* got *very* up close and personal, but she'd tried not to think about them rehearsing those scenes. She had to admit they made a ridiculously good-looking couple, and it sounded as if Ben was starting to be brainwashed by Dakota's pretty face. She was grateful when Hermione came over just in time to stop her from saying something stupid.

'Hey, guys,' said Hermione, her arms round her biology textbook. 'What's going on?' Abby noticed she was gripping the book fiercely, and not quite meeting Abby's eye.

'Not much!' said Abby. 'You OK? You seem a bit . . . tense?'

'I'm fine.' Hermione cleared her throat. 'Although, can I talk to you? Alone?'

'Um, sure,' said Abby, shrugging at Ben. 'Sorry!'

He grinned. 'No worries – catch you later!' Abby couldn't help but notice that he was heading towards Dakota and her crew who were doing a stupid break-dancing competition on the other side of the hall.

'So what's up, H?' asked Abby, her face clouding over as she noticed how upset her friend looked. 'OMG, are you OK? What's happened?'

Hermione looked at her angrily. 'I think you know.'

'I honestly don't!' said Abby, confused. 'Tell me, please! Is it something I've said? Is it something about the channel?' She knew that she'd been using up some of the best ideas for her vlogs, but she had been meaning to share some more group themes at the next meeting, and, besides, didn't Hermione enjoy doing book hauls?

'No, it's not the channel, it's the fact that you were blatantly copying my answers in that test,' snapped Hermione. 'I saw you, Abby!'

'What?' said Abby, taken completely by surprise. She thought she'd been so subtle, and Hermione hadn't given any sign of noticing. 'I – er – why would you think that?' she continued, floundering.

Hermione raised her voice. 'Look, I know what I saw, OK? Stop lying – it's pathetic! I revised for that test for the whole of Sunday afternoon.'

Abby squirmed, unsure whether to deny the accusations or confess everything. She knew that her lying was making Hermione even angrier, but for some reason she couldn't bring herself to tell the truth. 'I er . . . I revised too! Maybe I glanced your way but accidentally . . . I'm not really sure.'

'You're not sure?' challenged Hermione. There was a long, painful silence. 'Well, fine, if that's how you're going to play it.' She gave Abby a final look of disgust then walked off. Abby stared after her, her heart in her mouth. This was bad. Really bad. She wanted to go home and hide under the duvet.

Unfortunately that wasn't an option and Abby soldiered on for the rest of the day, her face burning every time she remembered Hermione's words. What if Hermione told their teacher? She handed in the English essay to Miss Piercy without having had a chance to work on it any more. Luckily, she wasn't needed for the *Grease* rehearsal today so she could go straight home. She had a vlog to prepare, but not before having a good cry.

VLOG 4

Amazing Abby: A Few of My Favourite Things Tag

4:05

FADE IN: ABBY'S BEDROOM

ABBY sits on her bed in jeans and white T-shirt, no make-up. WEENIE is curled up beside her, his chin resting in her lap.

ABBY

Hey, everybody! It's time for another video. I hope you enjoyed Lucy's cute farmyard vlog at the weekend, and thanks for the fantastic response to my truth or dare with Prankingstein.

Some of it was majorly embarrassing – wasn't it, Weenie? –
but we'll definitely do one again soon.

So, it was a tough day at school today and I thought it might be
a good time to try the A Few of My Favourite Things challenge.
I'm hoping it will cheer me up and entertain all of you too! It's a
tag video, which was invented by Victoria @inthefrow but lots of
famous YouTubers have done it. You have to name three of your
favourite things in twenty categories within three minutes – so
it's really, really fast and snappy. No time for my usual babbling!

(laughs)

And it's totally unscripted so who knows?

I've got the list of questions here.

(points to phone)

And I'm going to set the stopwatch. OK, let's get started!

ABBY (CONTINUED)

One: *products*. Hmmm . . . my iPhone, my Macbook Air and my
hair straighteners.

Two: *foods*. Oh, this is hard . . . I can't choose . . . but I have to, so I'll go for macaroni cheese, brownies and pizza. Healthy!

Three: *places*. Orlando, Florida – you know, Disney World – Ibiza, Spain and, ummm, Paris! Although I do love London too.

Four: *things you'd miss*. Weenie! My phone, obvs. And my friends. Oops, maybe I should have said my family?

Five: *things you do when you're bored*. Easy! Go on YouTube, cruise the fridge aaaand try out make-up!

Six: *things to do when it's sunny*. OK, sunbathe in my garden, go to the beach and eat ice cream – my favourite flavour at the moment is Caramel Crunch.

Seven: *films*.

(pauses for a few seconds)

OMG! Brain freeze . . . This is really hard. All of the Hunger Games films, *Mean Girls* (I know it's an old one but it's SO good) and *The Fault in Our Stars*? Oh wait, but I also love *If I Stay, Clueless* and *10 Things I Hate About You* . . . wait and *The Lion King*!

(throws her hands up in desperation)

It's impossible to pick three.

Eight: *songs*.

(sighs)

This is just as tough . . . not sure I can remember any actual song titles . . . basically anything by Taylor Swift, One Direction and Little Mix.

Nine: *brands*. Topshop . . . then maybe MAC (not that I can afford it – but I love trying the testers), um . . . and Starbucks?

Ten: *outdoor things you like*. Beaches, playing in the snow and, uh, water-skiing!

Eleven: *events*. Christmas, of course! Halloween and my birthday. Obvs.

Twelve: *cartoons. The Simpsons, SpongeBob* . . . my mind's gone blank . . . *Family Guy.*

Thirteen: *buildings.* This one's a bit random . . . but let me think. Um, the Eiffel Tower, the Empire State Building and . . . my house!

Fourteen: *anything in everyday life.* OMG! I don't know? Weenie, of course!
(gives WEENIE a kiss)
Hanging out with my friends and . . . and . . . new subscribers to our channel! Shout-out to any of you watching!

Fifteen: *traits in a person, not just partners.* Funny, loyal and uh, crazy! In a good way.

Sixteen: *influences.* YouTubers, Taylor Swift and . . . my mum! Is that embarrassing? But it's true – she's an amazing career woman who manages this huge team.

Seventeen: *drinks*. Easy! Smoothies, milkshakes and hot chocolate.

Eighteen: *experiences*. Disney World, swimming with dolphins and meeting RedVelvet. Actually I should have started with meeting RedVelvet!

Nineteen: *things to watch*. Do they mean *anything*? Then the answer is . . . YouTube, YouTube, YouTube! Plus musicals like *Wicked* and reality TV like *The Only Way is Essex* and *Made in Chelsea*.

Twenty: *YouTubers*. So many to choose from! I love them all. RedVelvet obvs, Zoella and Joe Suggs . . . oh, no, to be loyal it would have to be Prankingstein! Woo! That was intense.

How did I do?

(checks stopwatch)

Just under three minutes!

(fist pump)

So that was loads of fun for me, and has totally cheered me up. Now it's your turn! Instead of tagging any specific people I'm going to nominate *all* of you.

(points at camera)

Be sure to leave a link in the comments below so I can see your answers, and remember to tag other people! Let's keep this chain going!

Thanks for watching. Don't forget to give it a big thumbs-up and don't forget to subscribe. Bye.

ABBY waves.

FADE OUT.

Views: 327 and counting

Subscribers: 350

Comments:

MagicMorgan: Wow! This is gonna be my next video for sure.

LucyLocket: Love, love, love ♥ ♥ ♥

PrankingsteinCharlie: Thanks for the tag – I'm doing this next week 👍

ShyGirl1: I'm so bad at picking faves . . . Couldn't do it.

girlscanvlogfan: 3 things when I'm bored? Girls Can Vlog, Girls Can Vlog, Girls Can Vlog ☺

pink_sprinkles: 3 fave foods . . . cupcakes, cookies and mince pies xx

queen_dakota: 3 suggestions of when to stop making videos: now, immediately, yesterday

(scroll down to see 65 more comments)

Chapter Five

The main hall was stuffy and sweltering as a dozen conversations went on simultaneously, the odd phrase emanating loudly from the buzz of the room.

'It's very heartening to see how far Lucy has come in just a few short weeks,' beamed Mrs Harris, the history teacher. 'Her confidence has soared and she is engaging well with discussions in class. Great job, Lucy!' Abby glanced over as Lucy smiled bashfully at the next table, flanked by her proud-looking parents.

'Abby? Did you hear what Miss Piercy said, darling?' Abby tuned back in to her own Parents' Evening discussion and noticed with a start that her mother and

Miss Piercy were both looking at her expectantly.

Help!

'Um, yeah, the thing about my Shakespeare essay, right?' she said hopefully. 'I know, it really wasn't my greatest work. Sorry, I am trying harder, I swear!'

She cleared her throat nervously and glanced back at Lucy who was still being showered with praise. She wished that she and her friends were somewhere else, anywhere but here, talking about something other than stupid schoolwork and deadlines. Why couldn't the teachers and parents just talk to each other without her? Wasn't it enough that she showed up at school every day?

'Miss Piercy was suggesting that perhaps you have too much on your plate at the moment,' said her mum. 'And I'm a bit concerned that you can't even seem to stay focused on this very conversation!' Abby could tell that her mum was getting irritated from the way she was tapping her elegantly manicured nails on her designer iPad case. 'You'll be sitting your GCSEs before you know it. This is the time to really make an effort and it's not just English that's the problem – *all* your teachers seem concerned.'

Abby sighed in frustration. Her German and science meetings had been pretty cringe inducing, but what nobody seemed to realize was that she *was* making an effort. The cheating in biology had been a one-off, carried out in desperation, and totally not worth the humiliation that it had entailed. Even if Hermione had apparently refrained from telling the teacher, she was still avoiding Abby like the plague, which was almost worse. But Abby *did* often revise for other tests. She didn't expect to be top of the class like Hermione, but she didn't understand why her marks were so terrible. Even Kayleigh performed better than her, the girl who once asked their teacher what a potato tree looked like! Whatever Abby did, it never seemed enough to keep her head above water.

'As Abby's form teacher, I've had a chat with my colleagues and it sounds as if she's struggling in other subjects too,' said Miss Piercy, crossing her legs, clad in fuchsia tights.

Excellent footwear, Miss P! thought Abby, glancing at her teacher's gold T-bar shoes under the desk.

'We're wondering if there is something else awry here, aside from Abby's commitment to *Grease* and her, um, vlogging, er, hobby,' continued the teacher carefully.

'Yes, the YouTube stuff. Do you think that's a problem?' asked Mrs Pinkerton sharply, causing Abby to flinch. 'Abby has been doing a great deal of it recently.'

'Not "a great deal", Mum!' protested Abby, squirming. She looked at her teacher. 'It doesn't even take up that much time, miss, honestly.'

The teacher smiled. 'Even with all the clever editing you girls do?' Miss Piercy was the teacher who was most up to date with their YouTube activities, which was usually a good thing – but not today, apparently. 'That must be very time-consuming.'

'It's not that bad,' said Abby defensively. 'The videos

are only short, and we take turns making them.'

'That's enough, Abby,' said her mother, looking at the teacher. 'So you think we should put a stop to it?'

'Well, it's definitely worth considering which extra-curricular activities Abby could put on hold for the moment,' said Miss Piercy delicately. 'Just temporarily, Abby, and, as well as this, it might be an idea to put Abby forward for some . . . tests. Nothing to worry about, just something to look into, if you are both in agreement, of course.'

'What tests?' said Abby and her mother in unison.

Miss Piercy smiled. 'I'm not an expert, and neither are my colleagues, but there are various learning difficulties to be aware of.' She paused. 'If it's all right with you, we'd like to make an appointment for Abby with the educational psychologist for an initial assessment.'

Learning difficulties? Abby felt her stomach contract and her cheeks catch alight. *Educational psychologist?* Did this mean she was stupid?

*

The shock of Miss Piercy's suggestion was later eased by a good meeting with Ms Kusama who said she'd been pleased by how hard Abby had worked to catch up after joining *Grease* late in the day.

'She's really impressed me with her tenacity,' praised the teacher.

But it wasn't enough to put Abby's mum's mind at rest. 'To be honest, Abby, I wonder if *Grease* is too much of a commitment at this stage. I'm very proud to hear Ms Kusama's comments, and I know you love being in the show, but should you be learning all those lines when you could be revising or writing essays?'

Abby looked up from texting Ben.

19.41

Abby: Parents Evening disaster!!

'I can't quit now, Mum – I was the stand-in for Kayleigh: there's no one to replace *me*! Plus I've already learnt my lines.' She stared angrily out of the window. 'Anyway, you heard Miss Piercy. They think I'm thick – it's nothing to do with *Grease*.' She knew she was being immature, but she couldn't help it. The thought of seeing a psychologist made her feel sick.

Mrs Pinkerton patted Abby's arm. 'Darling, you're not thick, believe me. Don't be dramatic. It's just a case of managing your workload and your priorities, which is something you'll need to know how to do for the rest of your life!' She looked at her daughter's woebegone face as Abby miserably tapped out another message. 'Look, let's agree that you can stay in *Grease* – it sounds as if you're doing really well. But I think we're going to have to limit your time with that device, and put a lid on your videos for the time being.'

Abby looked up in despair. 'What device? *My phone?* I can't live without it, Mum! And that's not fair about the vlogging – Josh gets to do it.'

Mrs Pinkerton drummed her thumbs on the steering wheel, waiting for the traffic to clear. 'It's a different story for your brother and Prankingstein because his grades are fine – it's obvious from what Miss Piercy said that you can't afford to be distracted by YouTube right now.' She looked at Abby. 'I'm very proud of what you do, sweetheart, but we need to find a way to get you to focus.'

'But I've committed to making regular videos – it's our Girls Can Vlog pact!' protested Abby.

Her mum sighed. 'Look, I'm sure the girls can manage without you for a few weeks. It's a wonderful hobby, and if we see an improvement in your grades you can start doing it again. But for now *Grease* is more than enough. I'm going to need to report back to your father about what your teachers have said and I'm sure he will agree with my decision.'

'This is awful – I'll have no friends and no life.' Abby couldn't believe what was happening. 'You have to give me something to live for!'

Mrs Pinkerton rolled her eyes and returned her attention to the road. 'All right, drama queen, you can have your phone for an hour a day after school, and more at weekends so that you can keep in touch with your friends. I'm not a complete witch – I understand what you kids are like. But your education has to be our top priority. You can't afford to damage your future prospects.'

Abby listened in silence, defeated, reading Ben's reply as it pinged up on her phone.

20.02

> **Ben:** What's up?? Dakota said she saw u looking stressed in there.

Oh great! Just what she needed, proof that Ben and Dakota had been talking about her. She felt too depressed to respond. Ben would soon stop texting when her phone was taken away and she couldn't reply for hours on end . . . She bet Dakota always answered him in seconds. Urgh. Admittedly this wasn't as bad as when Lucy got her camera confiscated by the head after Dakota set her up in assembly, but the future wasn't exactly looking rosy right now.

And vlogging or no vlogging, she was about to be diagnosed as OFFICIALLY STUPID.

'So yeah, it wasn't too bad – I got brownie points from Mr Evans for the gymnastics coaching I've been doing at lunch,' Jessie was saying. 'Sort of cancelled out my awful history grades.'

Abby approached the table as her friends were mid-Parents' Evening debrief.

'How'd it go for you, Abs?' asked Jessie.

Abby sat down and started fiddling with a sachet of ketchup. 'Er, no brownie points for me but, you know . . .' She glanced up. Hermione was glaring at her, but the others hadn't noticed. Abby attempted a breezy laugh. 'Parents' Evening, it's meant to be rubbish, right?'

'T-totally,' said Lucy. 'Anyway, enough about that boring topic of conversation, why don't we c-catch up on GCV stuff instead . . . w-we need to brainstorm the next few videos. Hermione, you've got that b-baking one lined up, right, and then, Abs, were we going

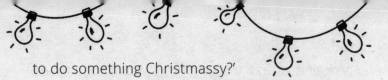

to do something Christmassy?'

Abby shook the sachet. 'Yep . . . why isn't this stuff coming out?'

'Maybe a sh-shopping trip?' suggested Lucy. 'For presents?'

'Mm-hm.' Abby continued to shake the sachet, killing time, until she realized the others were all looking at her expectantly (apart from Hermione, who was still shooting daggers). She sighed. There was no getting out of this – she had to be straight with them. 'Sounds good, Luce, but there's actually something I need to say to you guys.'

'Ooh!' said Jessie. 'Sounds interesting.'

'Not really, I'm afraid,' Abby mumbled. 'As chairperson, I'm going to rely on your support for the coming weeks. I'm sort of . . . not allowed . . . to vlog right now. For a few weeks, actually. Or maybe even months.'

'What – cos you were flirting with Charlie in that Prankingstein video?' said Jessie, eyes wide. 'Did your mum freak out?'

Abby laughed. Trust Jessie to come up with a completely bonkers theory! 'No, my mum knows that was just a bit of fun. Anyway, we weren't really flirting!'

'I don't know – he looked pretty d-disappointed when you k-kissed Weenie instead of him,' said Lucy.

'Do you think so?' asked Abby, eyes lighting up. 'What specifically made you think that?'

Hermione rolled her eyes impatiently. 'Never mind that, Abby. You were about to tell us why you're not allowed to vlog . . . ?'

Abby sighed. 'Yeah, so it's totally nothing to do with the vlogging itself – my mum thinks we're great – but . . . like . . .' She lowered her voice. 'I'm really messing up with school stuff, OK? My grades are terrible and I keep being told if I don't learn how to "focus" I'm going to blow my GCSEs. Literally, it's all I'm hearing: focus, focus, hashtag *focus*!' She shrugged and picked at her food. 'Anyway, I can still help with ideas and stuff, it's just I can't do any filming and I'm only allowed my phone for an hour a day.'

'Oh man – I f-feel your pain!' said Lucy. 'I didn't realize your grades were that b-bad, though?'

'Well, they're not *THAT* bad –' Abby broke off as she saw the look on Hermione's face. She had witnessed her F in English as well as the cheating in biology. 'Oh, who am I kidding, they're terrible! The worst! In pretty much EVERY subject regardless of how hard I try.' She pushed her plate away and crossed her arms. 'So now you know. Amazing Abby is a complete dunce! Always has been, always will be.'

There was an awkward silence. 'You are in n-no way a dunce, Abs,' said Lucy gently. 'You're the b-brains behind our entire operation! Our subscriber count has soared and it's all because of you.' Jessie nodded in agreement. 'And you're d-doing amazingly in *Grease*! As for your grades, not everyone is cut out for schoolwork, but who cares?'

'I care,' said Abby miserably. 'They're actually going to test me for learning difficulties. How embarrassing is that?' It was a relief to say it out loud and she almost laughed as she watched her friends try not to react to the phrase *learning difficulties*. Lucy was taking care not to look too surprised, Jessie was somewhat less successful at this, her eyebrows practically jumping off her face, and Hermione studied Abby carefully. 'I know, it's full on, right, guys? But, whatever happens, at least the teachers might cut me some slack,' she continued.

The bell rang. 'Glad you told us, Abs!' said Jessie. 'Gotta run to gymnastics practice but I can definitely help out with some extra vlogging, so let's talk later?'

'Yeah, I've got to go too, but I'll do m-more too, when I can,' said Lucy. '*Grease* and seeing Sam are taking up a lot of w-weekends right now, but we'll g-get it covered.'

'Thanks, guys – you're the best,' said Abby as Lucy and Jessie rushed off.

Hermione and Abby were left alone at the table. Abby picked up the ketchup sachet again, fiddled with it despondently, then put it down. She glanced up slowly. 'H – I owe you an apology – you were right about the test and I'm really sorry.'

Hermione continued to size her up, reminding Abby of a judge in a courtroom drama. Finally she asked, 'But why did you have to lie?'

'I don't know. I was desperate. Then I was so embarrassed when I realized you were on to me I didn't know what to say.' Abby looked at her pleadingly. 'I promise it won't happen again, ever.'

Hermione suddenly reached across the table and grabbed the ketchup sachet. 'There's a knack to this, you know. Here you go.' She shook the sauce on to Abby's chips, then looked up at her. 'Fine. You're forgiven. I can help you with some of your studying, if you want?'

'That would be great,' said Abby, grinning with relief. 'Wow, I really thought you hated me.'

Hermione gave a little shake of her head. 'Of course not.'

Abby leaned over and gave Hermione a hug. What would she do without her amazing friends?

To: TheRealRedVelvet100@gmail.com

From: amazingabby@abbys_world.com

Hey Tiffany,

Thanks for your comments on our vlogs – we're really glad you're watching! I'm actually writing to let you know that I'm going to be off the channel for a while. Soooo depressing but my grades are terrible right now so I need to concentrate on school. Which obviously sucks, big time! But the others are going to keep it going without me, which is totally awesome of them even if I can't help feeling left out.

Hope you're really well and give Bambi a cuddle for me!

Abby xoxo

PRANKINGSTEIN VLOG

Pranking Amazing Abby From GCV!!

6:45

FADE IN: ABBY'S FAMILY BATHROOM – DAY

JOSH is filming into the mirror, the bath and shower in shot behind him.

JOSH

Hi there, PrankingFans, thanks for tuning in! It's just me today . . . and I'm about to play a trick on my annoying younger sister Abby who always hogs the bathroom as if she owns it. For hours and hours *AND HOURS* – I mean, what does she even do in here? Anyway, now it's payback time!

JOSH holds up a bottle of conditioner.

JOSH (CONTINUED)
So here is Abby's favourite conditioner, which comes in this purple bottle and is actually purple. It's pretty expensive . . .

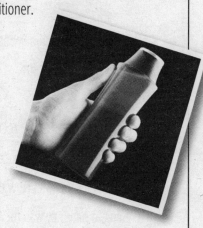

(laughs maniacally)
. . . and here I am dumping it down the sink.

CRAZY COLOUR

JOSH pours the contents down the sink. He then picks up another bottle that reads: CRAZY COLOUR.

JOSH (CONTINUED)

Now THIS is Crazy Colour, some very powerful hair dye, which is also purple. I am now going to pour it into the empty bottle.

JOSH fills up the conditioner bottle with the CRAZY COLOUR. He films the inside of the bottle.

JOSH (CONTINUED)

Impossible to tell the difference, right? I'm hoping Abby won't either until it's too late! Now that I've done the switcheroo, I'm going to patiently wait for Abby to have a shower, which she usually does when she comes home from school.

I'll keep you posted . . .

FADE TO BLACK.

FADE IN: ABBY'S HOUSE – UPSTAIRS HALLWAY

JOSH is standing outside the bathroom door.

JOSH

(whispers)

So Abby just got back from school and jumped into the shower.

She was not in the best of moods . . . so this could be interesting.

(giggles)

She is totally going to kill me! Don't worry, I won't film her in

the shower.

We hear water running.

ABBY

(screams from inside the bathroom)

EWW! What is this? Why is my hair turning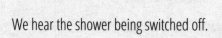

purple? It's purple EVERYWHERE!

We hear the shower being switched off.

JOSH

(knocks on the door)

Are you decent?

JOSH enters the bathroom and films ABBY, wrapped in a towel and looking into the mirror above the sink, holding a strand of wet but clearly purple hair.

ABBY

YOU HAVE GOT TO BE KIDDING ME! Josh! I know this was you! You are such a ridiculous human being! You need to get a life!

JOSH

Calm down, it's just a prank! It will wash out . . . eventually . . .

(laughs nervously)

Anyway, it kind of suits you!

ABBY

(shrieking, almost in tears)

You don't understand! I'm going to have to wash it a million times to get it out, or bleach it. What if it's not back to normal for the show? This is a disaster. Switch that camera off now! Is Mum home?

(shouts)

MUM! MUM! Come and see what your stupid son Josh has done to me!

JOSH

(to camera)

Time to make a quick exit, I think! If you enjoyed this Girls Can Vlog pranking special, give us a thumbs-up. Don't forget to subscribe and check out the Girls Can Vlog channel – all links are below. Byeee!

FADE OUT.

Subscribers: 4,234
Views: 1,546

Comments:

Amazing_Abby_xxx: I've uploaded this to the GCV channel too so that you guys can feel my pain!!!!! I'm SOOO angry!!!! 😠

lucylocket: OMG. You poor thing!

billythekid: LOL LOL LOL

jazzyjessie: Actually purple is kinda cool . . . and they can't tell you off at school.

ShyGirl1: So glad I don't have a brother 😮

StalkerGurl: Josh why are you so funny xx

peter_pranks: Hahahha nice one mate

PrankingsteinCharlie: What an idiot . . . Don't get angry – get even @Amazing_Abby_xxx. 😉

(scroll down to see 24 more comments)

Chapter Six

'Right, that's it, I give up!' Arms exhausted, Abby shook her hair out of the side ponytail and put down her hairbrush, spitting out kirby grips. It was the third look she'd tried, but however she styled it there was no getting away from the fact that her beloved pale-blonde hair was now purple. And not even a dark, elegant plummy purple. No. A violently vivid violet with pink hues. Some people could carry it off, but bold colours had never been her thing. 'Josh, I'm going to kill you,' she muttered. What if she didn't manage to get the dye out in time for the opening night of *Grease*? Frenchy was the character with colourful hair, not Jan! As if she didn't have enough to worry about at the moment.

Still, at least the video had gone down well with the GCV fans – a new surge of followers had subscribed, and Abby couldn't deny that she would have been gripped by the video too, if someone else had been the poor unknowing victim. She glanced at her watch and closed her locker. *Eek – nearly time for rehearsal.* Ignoring the looks she got as she dashed down the corridor, she arrived at the theatre breathlessly, only to find the rest of the cast walking offstage. 'Halftime break!' announced Ms Kusama. 'Well done, everybody. Take five.'

'Where've you been?' asked Lucy, rushing up to her. 'I was going to text you but I r-remembered you didn't have your phone. You weren't embarrassed about y-your hair, were you?'

'What? No!' said Abby. 'Everyone's seen it by now! I must have got the time wrong. How stupid of me.'

Ameeka sauntered past. 'Oh yeah . . . Ms Kusama moved rehearsal forward by an hour – the theatre was double-booked. I said I'd tell you, but then I forgot. Nice hair, though, babes.' As she walked over to Dakota without missing a beat, Abby rolled her eyes. Dakota gave her a sarcastic wave, before tapping something into her phone.

'Perfect. Just, perfect!' groaned Abby. 'Which scene did you rehearse?'

'The big opening number.' Lucy was still gazing after Ameeka. 'How is it p-possible for someone to be so mean? If you were a teacher, would you really trust her to p-pass on a message . . . about *anything?* Anyway, I think we're going to try the scene again after the break so d-don't worry.'

'Phew – that means I can go to the loo. I didn't think I'd have time.' Abby ran towards the chilly, ancient toilet backstage. 'Sorry, Ms Kusama!' she cried on her way. 'Back in a sec.'

Aware of Dakota's eyes still on her, she headed for the cubicle. *Brrr, why don't they install some heating in here?* she wondered, listening to the noise of someone moving furniture around backstage. As she went to open the door a few moments later, she froze. The door was stuck. She tried the handle again. Nothing.

'What the –?' she said out loud. As she tried a third time, she started to panic. Reaching for her phone in her skirt pocket she remembered with a shock that she didn't have it. She realized at the same time that the noises outside had stopped. 'HELLO?' she cried, thumping on the door. 'IS ANYONE THERE?'

Silence. Followed by what sounded like a gleeful snort.

'Who's there?' called Abby, perplexed. 'Can you let me out? I need to get back to rehearsal!' Her heart sunk as she heard footsteps walking away.

'HEY, COME BACK HERE,' yelled Abby, outraged. 'NOW!'

As the rehearsal music started up again, she realized that she had no hope of being heard. She sat back down on the toilet, her blood boiling. This was something Dakota and her stupid gang had done. What did they have against her anyway – was it revenge for taking

Kayleigh's part, or was this about Dakota and her dumb fixation with Ben? He'd been giving Dakota loads of attention recently as it was!

Abby sulkily examined the graffiti on the door. It was complete torture being stuck. She could just about hear the dialogue onstage and the exact moment where her line was supposed to come. Then the heavy pause when it wasn't delivered, followed by the noise of Ms Kusama's surprised voice chipping in when she realized that Abby still wasn't there. Abby muttered the line despondently in the toilet, 'Jeez, I wish it was still summer.'

Twenty minutes later, just as she was losing the will to live and the circulation in her hands seemed to have come to a complete standstill, she heard footsteps running up to the cubicle door.

'HELP! HELP!' Abby cried out desperately.

'Abby, are you in there? Wh-why is there a chair here?'

Relief swept over her. 'Lucy! Let me out!' she cried. 'I think someone wedged the door shut!'

'Someone what? Oh my god, h-hang on!' Within

seconds Lucy had moved the chair and Abby was free. 'Are you OK?' asked Lucy, hugging her friend tightly. 'Sorry I couldn't get away to look for you earlier – by the time I realized you hadn't come back we were mid-scene. You are having the w-worst day!'

'Don't worry. I'm just so happy to be out,' said Abby. 'Can you believe they did that to me though – hashtag *pathetic*!'

'Who do you think it was?' said Lucy, offering her some pick-'n'-mix. 'S-sugar for the shock!'

Abby gratefully accepted a handful. 'It might have been Kayleigh – there's no mistaking the elephant snort I heard. Maybe she wants her part back. But I think there's more to it – it's obvious Dakota wants me out of the way and it explains Ameeka not passing on the message about the new rehearsal time too. It's so pathetic that they don't have anything better to do!'

They walked back towards the theatre where most of the cast had dispersed and sat in the front row of the stalls. Dakota and Ben were rehearsing a Rizzo and Kenickie scene with Ms Kusama onstage.

'Sam's coming to meet me. I'd b-better go,' whispered Lucy. 'We're going ice skating. Will you be OK?'

'Of course,' said Abby absently, watching Dakota and Ben, whose characters were having a furious argument. Dakota shoved Ben with both hands – then smiled sweetly at him and high-fived him as she came out of character. 'I'm just going to . . . hang around for a bit,' she told Lucy. 'I need to apologize to Ms Kusama.'

'Apologize? But . . . aren't you going to explain what happened with D-Dakota?'

'Not yet,' whispered Abby, her eyes still fixed on the stage. 'I need more proof that she was behind it. For now I don't want to cause any trouble or give Ms Kusama any reason to chuck me off the show. She's literally the only teacher who believes in me right now. Say hi to Sam for me.'

'Will do. Sp-speak to you later!'

After Lucy had left, Abby tried to catch Ben's eye but he

was completely immersed in the scene, brushing off his jacket and giving 'Rizzo' an angry look as he stomped away.

'That's fantastic, guys!' said Ms Kusama. 'I'm loving your energy – I can really sense the tension fizzing between you.'

Ugh, thought Abby in disgust, getting out of her seat. *Fizzing tension? I can't stand this any more.* She decided to chat to Ms Kusama tomorrow.

'How's it going, Abs, or should I say Ribena Roots?' Abby jumped as Charlie caught up with her in the hallway outside the theatre.

'Har, har,' she said with a reluctant smile, touching her hair self-consciously. 'I can't believe you let my moron of a brother get away with this.' She hadn't run into Charlie since their truth-or-dare video and it felt really good to see him.

He held up his hands in mock outrage. 'I knew nothing about it, I swear! But, come to think of it, I think the colour kind of suits you. I mean, the purple Teletubby was always my favourite, and Barney the dinosaur is, like, a complete legend. Go Team Purple!'

Abby poked her tongue out at him. 'What are you doing here, anyway?'

'Meeting with Ms K. I'm going to help out with the lighting for *Grease* so I'll be attending most of your rehearsals from now on.'

Abby felt her heart leap. 'That's so cool! It's a fun production. I have no idea what I'm supposed to do if I can't wash out this dye, though. Wish I could get Josh back for this, but I can't think of anything good.'

'Well, don't panic,' said Charlie, his eyes lighting up. 'After all, who's the perfect person to help you? The person who knows Josh's every movement, his every fear . . . the person who is excellently trained at pranks, the person who is currently standing next to a violet-haired beauty . . .'

Abby giggled, ideas suddenly flooding her mind. 'You want to help me plan a revenge prank? Yes! This is the best news I've had all day!'

When she got home, Abby was merrily plotting what she and Charlie could cook up when her phone – hers for sixty whole blissful minutes – pinged loudly.

16.02

Ben: Sorry we didn't get to chat today – hope u're ok xx

She smiled, rereading the message and cradling the phone in her hands. Did he know what Dakota had done, or was he just curious about why Abby had missed rehearsal? Either way, he was thinking about her, not his intimate scene with Dakota, and she chalked that up to another win.

16.04

Abby: Ben sent me a message!! Two kisses! Sorry, Dakota, but your plan just keeps FAILING.

16.05

Lucy: Haha! He clearly really likes you and D can't change that. What's she going to do, lock you in your bedroom for seventy years? Xx

16.06

Abby: Argh! Don't tempt fate! 😲

VLOG 6

FADE IN: SHOPPING CENTRE – DAY

LUCY, SAM, HERMIONE and JESSIE are huddled with takeaway hot chocolates on a bench in their local shopping mall.

LUCY

Hi, Girls Can Vlog fans! It's nearly D-December which means a) time for hot chocolate and b) it's officially time to start Christmas sh-shopping! So we thought we'd vlog our first

attempt at this – it's so exciting that Sam has agreed to
overcome his fear of social media and j-join us, especially as
Abby can't make it today.

JESSIE

(from behind camera)

Sam, you do look pretty similar to Abby, come to think of it.

SAM

Ha ha! Hi, everyone!

SAM waves awkwardly.

JESSIE

(from behind the camera)

He's Lucy's boyfriend, in case you didn't know!

HERMIONE

Shall we get started? I've got soooo much shopping to do . . .

Can we hit a bookshop first? Pretty please?

LUCY

It's shopping for other people, remember, l-little bookworm?
Actually, we're right in front of L-Lush so let's pop in there first.
They've got so many fabulous things, perfect for gifts. And I like
that it's cruelty free and not tested on animals . . .

HERMIONE

OK, as long as we go book shopping later . . .

We see LUCY, SAM and HERMIONE walking into Lush. JESSIE is
filming. Pan over the shop from entrance.

JESSIE

(from behind the camera)

Ooh, it smells sooo
good and it's laid out so
beautifully – I just wanna
buy everything! Let's look
at the bath bombs and
bubble baths . . . they make great stocking stuffers.

HERMIONE

Can someone get that funny flamingo-shaped bubble bar for

me? It's so cute!

LUCY

Yummy! This one is glittery and smells like b-bubblegum. I'm

sure Maggie would love it! Here, Sam, smell this!

LUCY shoves the bath bomb into SAM's face. He recoils.

SAM

Urggh! You won't catch me putting that in my bath!

LUCY laughs.

LUCY

OK, let's move over to the
make-up. I want to get
some n-nail polishes too.

HERMIONE, JESSIE and LUCY move over to the make-up counters.

JESSIE

(from behind the camera)

Sam, come here! I need your help . . .

SAM saunters up to JESSIE at one of the make-up counters. She takes a large brush, dabs it in some glittery powder and then suddenly brushes it all over SAM's cheeks.

JESSIE (CONTINUED)

(laughing hysterically)

Perfect! It really suits you!

SAM

Jeeeesss! Yuck!

SAM frantically tries to brush the glitter dust off his face.

SAM (CONTINUED)

(laughing)

You lot are so annoying! Lucy, sorry, but I'm out of here!

SAM manages to get Jessie back with the glitter dust before racing out of the shop.

CUT TO: CLAIRE'S ACCESSORIES – LATER

JESSIE is still filming.

JESSIE

So now we're in Claire's Accessories for a quick browse . . . and we've lost Sam. He couldn't take it any more – he's gone back to the cafe.

JESSIE films herself trying on sunglasses and hats.

JESSIE (CONTINUED)

Check out this Justin Bieber

singing toothbrush! How amazing is that!

HERMIONE

Look at this really pretty owl
necklace. It's so delicate. Anyone
want to give it to me? Hint, hint!
Oh, and look at these amazing
dangly earrings. These might be
nice for someone we know?

LUCY

Let's see. Ooh, yes. I think she'd l-love them. Oh, look there's a
ten for ten pounds offer on rings and hair accessories!

LUCY, HERMIONE and JESSIE look at lots of small items and put
some in their basket.

JESSIE

We're going to clean out the shop! Too many fabulous things
and too little money . . . And we still need to get to Topshop!

LUCY

Poor Sam. He'll be on his f-fourth hot chocolate by now! I'll just go check on him . . .

CUT TO: LUCY'S BEDROOM – LATER

All three girls are sprawled on the bed with shopping bags, bowls of popcorn and crisp packets.

LUCY

So we just got home from sh-shopping and our arms are tired from carrying all our goodies! Amazing success! I'm totally b-broke now!

JESSIE

Let's dump it all on the bed and have a look. But first I need a snack – I'm starving!

HERMIONE

Actually we can't show you everything as CERTAIN PEOPLE will be watching our video even though we warned them not to!

JESSIE

Yeah, yeah, who cares! I can't wait any more . . .

JESSIE empties all the bags on to the bed while munching away on a handful of popcorn.

LUCY

Love the s-smell of those bath bombs! Don't you like it,

Foghorn?

FOGHORN the cat jumps
off the bed and strolls
away in disgust.

LUCY (CONTINUED)

I guess it's a bit

overpowering!

HERMIONE

And here are all the amazing nail polishes – silver, bronze and

purple glitter. Confession – I bought a couple for myself . . .

and these tinted lip balms were buy one get one free.

JESSIE

I got a load of cute socks with pandas, penguins, owls . . . and

this adorable penguin hat for my baby brother!

JESSIE models a silly baby hat.

HERMIONE

I love this Hunger Games T-shirt – not sure who it's for yet . . . And I got this Christmas candle with pine needles in it for my mum. I'm pretty sure she won't be watching!

LUCY

I got something really fabulous for Sam, not saying what in case he's watching – but it might help keep his ears w-warm at the City Farm this winter!

(she giggles)

OK, I think we might be running out of time so l-let's wind it up.

JESSIE

But I've got more stuff!

LUCY

Save it for next time! So, g-guys, we hope you really enjoyed this video and that it's helped to get you in a Christmassy mood! Give us a thumbs-up b-below, and see you soon!

JESSIE, HERMIONE and LUCY

(waving)

Bye-eee!

FADE OUT.

Views: 538

Subscribers: 497

Comments:

Amazing_Abby_xxx: Wish I'd been there! Looks like sooo much fun.

xxrainbowxx: I can't believe how much money you spent! I'm poor ☹

StephSaysHi: Don't be mean – you're just jel! They probably saved up.

glitzygirl: You guys are awesome! #friendshipgoals

pink_sprinkles: I'm a Lush addict too! ❤

MagicMorgan: I'm doing a Christmas shopping haul too 🎄

(scroll down for 73 more comments)

Chapter Seven

18.52

Lucy: So, I'm not dreaming – that was definitely Ben we saw with Dakota in the cafe outside Lush! 😲

18.53

Hermione: Yeah. Didn't realize those two met up outside school?

18.56

Jessie: I do NOT trust him.

18.57

Lucy: He's been texting Abs – like, a lot. Should we say something?

18.58

Hermione: Maybe. She's really into him . . .

18.59

Jessie: Yeah, and I think D&B were holding hands? 😔

19.00

Lucy: Oh no. Poor Abby . . . 😮

As Abby waited to see the psychologist with her mum, she felt sick with nerves, regretting her decision to make one of RedVelvet's trademark green smoothies for breakfast. Even now she could feel the apple and kiwi juices sloshing about unpleasantly in her stomach.

'Everything will be fine, Abby,' said her mum, giving

her smartphone a final check before switching it off and reaching for her daughter's hand. She looked preoccupied, a wrinkle denting her smooth forehead, but this wasn't uncommon – being the editor one of the country's best-selling fashion magazines meant that she was often a million miles away, brainstorming a new cover look for the magazine or deciding which of her competitors' writers to poach next.

Mr McClafferty, the balding headmaster, poked his head round the door and ushered them into his office.

'Do come in, and thank you for waiting,' he said. 'You remember Mrs Monroe.' The psychologist, a friendly middle-aged woman with auburn hair and bright red lipstick rose from her chair and shook hands with Abby's mum. Abby had met Mrs Monroe when she was being interviewed and taking the tests last week. She'd seemed like a warm and positive person, but Abby hadn't enjoyed the experience, nor the physical exam with the paediatrician.

'Hello, Mrs Pinkerton. Hello again, Abby,' said Mrs

Monroe. 'Thank you for coming today to have a chat.'

'No problem,' said Abby's mum, cheerfully brisk as they took their seats. 'So, what's going on, exactly? Abby here is a little worried, but I'm sure there's nothing to panic about.'

Abby winced. 'Mum, I told you, I'm fine. Let's just get this over with, OK?' She was trying to behave like she wasn't bothered, but her mum was ruining her carefree act.

The psychologist smiled. 'There's nothing to be anxious about. In fact, this investigation and possible diagnosis is a positive step for Abby in that we can work out what is best for her moving forward.' Abby noticed her mum sit up at the word 'diagnosis'.

'The doctor's examination showed that Abby is healthy and doesn't have any physical problems, which is good news,' continued Mrs Monroe. 'The various test results have eliminated a lot of possible conditions, such as dyslexia and dyspraxia. But my observations and statements from Abby's teachers suggest that she may have a minor form of ADHD, which stands for attention deficit hyperactivity disorder.'

The words floated past Abby. She heard her mother stifle a gasp, covering it up by clearing her throat. Was it terrible? Was she disappointed? Shocked? She stared at the slightly wilting flowers on Mr McClafferty's bookshelf.

Mrs Monroe smiled sympathetically. 'It's not uncommon at all. We think it's caused by developmental differences in the brain that affect the parts controlling attention, concentration, impulsivity, activity levels and memory. We will need to continue to observe Abby, but now we can start to take steps to make sure that Abby's education and studying can be more carefully tailored to her needs. There's a lot that can be done with behavioural therapy and learning simple study skills.' Her smile got even bigger, as if she was telling them they'd won the lottery. 'As I say, this is a big positive!'

'Well . . . yes, absolutely,' said Abby's mum after a pause. 'A huge positive, really.'

Suddenly, Abby was overwhelmed with irritation. 'You don't think it's a positive, Mum. No need to lie about it. I've got something wrong with me and now I need to have special help. Not what every parent wants to hear, is it? I bet you're dreading telling Dad.'

Mrs Monroe's smile finally faltered and she exchanged anxious glances with Mr McClafferty.

Abby's mum looked at her in surprise. 'Abby, I can see you're upset, but there's no need to be rude. We'll deal with this in the best way we can. The main thing is that you'll be getting the help you need.' She lowered her voice. 'And, yes, your father needs to know, because he's interested in your education – even if you don't get to see him very often.'

Abby fixed her glare on the vase of flowers and took a couple of angry breaths. She felt bad for embarrassing her mum. 'Sorry,' she muttered. 'I know you guys are there for me – I'm just really hating this whole thing.'

'It's completely natural for you to feel like that,' Mrs

Monroe told Abby patiently, her smile back. 'But please listen to what we have to suggest and I'm sure you will start to see how it can help you take back control.'

11.03

> **Lucy:** Guys, I saw B&D together in an empty classroom at break – there's def something going on.

11.05

> **Jessie:** What were they doing?

11.07

> **Lucy:** He was playing with her hair, and they were standing really close together 😖

11.07

> **Jessie:** VERY COSY.

11.08

> **Lucy:** Think I have to tell Abs . . .

11.09

Hermione: Yeah, she needs to know. 😞

11.10

Jessie: Agree x

11.11

Lucy: Btw, Jess, you still OK to do a vlog this week? x

11.12

Jessie: YES! BEEN PLANNING IT! CANNOT WAIT!!!

'Brr, it's freezing! Too cold for PE and too c-cold for these stupid skirts!' said Lucy as she and Abby walked from the changing rooms to the netball courts. 'So, s-spill – where were you in English this m-morning?'

Abby grimaced. She'd avoided telling her friends about the latest developments – one good thing about her phone ban. But there was no point in hiding the diagnosis, and she knew Lucy wouldn't judge her anyway.

'I had my appointment . . . you know, for what I told you about after Parents' Evening?' Lucy nodded. 'Yeah, so I got hashtag *assessed* last week then today my mum came in for this meeting . . . and it turns out I have ADHD. Basically I have trouble concentrating and stuff. Who knew, right?' She laughed a little uneasily, glancing quickly at Lucy to see her reaction.

'Well, that doesn't sound so bad,' said Lucy, linking arms with her. 'Lots of p-people in my old school had that. What can they d-do about it?'

Abby shrugged. 'It's kinda boring . . . I've got to have these special lessons to help me learn to study more effectively and . . . Oh, hey, Ben!' Ben was waving at her as he ran towards the running track and she was relieved at the change of subject.

'Hey, Abby!' he called, slowing down and jogging on the spot. 'Nice legs!'

'Back at you!' shouted Abby, her face lighting up. 'Enjoy the workout – no slacking!'

He laughed. 'Yes, coach, I'm aiming for my personal

best! See you later, babe.'

'"Hi, Lucy, n-nice to see you, Lucy",' joked Lucy as he picked up speed again and ran off. 'Again, am I invisible?'

Abby laughed. 'Ben's being really sweet right now. The one good thing in my life, well, apart from you guys, I mean. I know he likes me . . . Did you hear him call me babe?'

'Yeah . . . but, do you actually like him?' asked Lucy cautiously. 'Like, p-properly?'

Why is she looking so serious? wondered Abby.

'Totally,' she replied out loud. 'He's been sending me the funniest texts, and there's definitely chemistry between us.' She snapped her gum. 'I mean, nothing's actually happened yet. I'm kind of waiting for him to make a move, you know?' Lucy shrugged. 'Maybe at the first-night cast party?' Abby giggled. 'Anyway, how did you know when Sam was going to kiss you? Could you tell – or wait! Were you the one to lunge at him?' She put her arm round her friend's shoulder and pulled her in tight. 'You never tell me ANYTHING!'

Lucy laughed. 'I did tell you – not much of a story – he k-kissed me by a pond! I think we both kind of lunged at the s-same time . . . I can't really remember.'

'Sooo cute,' said Abby. 'But not helpful to me in my current predicament. I just don't know if Ben is the kind of guy who likes it when the girl makes the first move.'

'He's definitely been f-flirting with you,' Lucy said slowly. 'But isn't he quite, er, *friendly* with loads of people? Well, not me obviously! But, you know, other g-girls?'

Abby glanced at her in surprise. 'Yeah, I mean, he's a complete charmer, but . . . there's more than that between us. Remember, I showed you his texts?' She mentally ran through them again. 'He's totally into me – I know it!'

'Yeah, it does seem like that. It's just that . . . well, be c-careful.'

Abby's brow wrinkled in confusion. 'Careful?' *About what?*

Lucy sighed. 'OK, so there's something I need to tell you, Abs. We were out shopping at the weekend and—'

'LOOK WHO IT IS!' boomed Kayleigh, interrupting her as they approached the netball court. 'L-L-L Lucy Lockjaw and her purple-haired special-needs friend Amazing Abby.' The other girls on court all stopped their stretching and stared.

Abby froze in horror as Dakota burst out laughing. 'Kayleigh, you are so bad – I love it!' Then she shivered, already bored with the subject. 'Urgh, why is it so freaking cold out here?'

'Is it true you're staying back a year, Abby?' drawled Ameeka, taking off her sweatshirt and throwing it at Dakota. 'There you go, babe. I'm kind of warm.'

'What are you talking about, Ameeka?' hissed Abby. 'I'm not staying back a year.' She marched over to Kayleigh and grabbed her by the arm. 'Why did you call me that? Special needs?'

'Don't deny it. I saw you and your mum walking out of the office with Mrs Monroe this morning,' said Kayleigh, projecting her voice like a booming Shakespearean actor. Some of the girls saw what she was trying to do, and pretended to ignore her – but Abby knew they were all listening. 'Let's just say your poor mum wasn't wearing the face of a proud parent.'

Ouch, thought Abby. *Can't argue with that.*

'As if you would even know what a proud parent looked like, Kayleigh,' said Jessie, walking over angrily. 'Why can't you just leave people alone?'

To Abby's relief the teacher showed up before the situation got any worse, and started barking orders at the class. Abby felt really hurt by Kayleigh's words, and embarrassed that everyone knew her business before she'd had a chance to process it herself. She hadn't even told Jessie and Hermione anything yet. Still, it helped to know that Lucy understood what she was going through – she'd had to fight her own battles over teasing about her stammer when she'd started at the school. It had been really rough on her, but now people hardly ever mentioned it.

'Hey, Luce, what were you about to tell me before Kayleigh opened her stupid mouth?' she said as they lined up to collect their balls.

'Just that at the weekend – er, no, d-doesn't matter,' said Lucy, looking at her anxious-faced friend. Now was definitely not the time. 'Come on, let's shoot some hoops!'

VLOG 7

FADE IN: JESSIE'S BEDROOM – DAY

JESSIE is under the bright turquoise zebra-striped duvet in her bedroom. An alarm clock on her bedside table rings. She comes out from under the duvet, switches it off and ducks down under duvet again. The alarm rings for a second time and this time she sits up and stretches.

JESSIE

Guess it's time to get up! Too bad – I was having such a good dream . . .

JESSIE does a forward roll out of the bed then cartwheels across her floor.

JESSIE (CONTINUED)

(from behind camera)

So, hi, guys! Today it's my turn to host Girls Can Vlog and I thought I'd show you my morning routine . . .

(pans around the room)

This is my lovely bedroom, which just got a makeover. I love the colours and the bright lighting – perfect for filming.

JESSIE slips into a pair of fuzzy dinosaur-feet slippers and lifts up her foot to show one off.

JESSIE (CONTINUED)

Cute, aren't they? Anyway, off to the bathroom to get ready.

MOVE TO: JESSIE'S BATHROOM

JESSIE (CONTINUED)

Wish I had my very own bathroom, but no such luck! I need to fight my way through my baby brother's rubber ducks and toys, which are everywhere! Not to mention my older brother's gross razors . . . So first I brush my teeth. Since I got braces last year I've had to be really careful about keeping them clean.

CLOSE UP: JESSIE grinning at camera.

JESSIE (CONTINUED)

I have to be careful eating sweets too, which is a huge pain –
no gummy bears, gum or toffees for me, boohoo! But on the
plus side it's fun to play with the rubber bands and to flick
them at people – kinda accidentally on purpose!

(laughs)

Then I wash my face and put on moisturizer, but otherwise I
don't wear any make-up. Apart from the odd dab of lip balm,
sometimes, but I'm not a girly girl as you can probably tell. My
hair is in braids, which means I don't have to do much else to
it, although I have to get the braids done at the hairdressers
every two months and it takes AGES!

CUT TO: JESSIE'S BEDROOM

JESSIE's outfit is laid out on the bed.

JESSIE

My outfit for today is my fave skinny jeans and this awesome hoodie that
I got recently. Plus leopard-print socks and Converse. I'll be back . . .

CUT TO: JESSIE in her bedroom, now dressed.

JESSIE

I'm absolutely starving so gonna hurry down to breakfast.

JESSIE runs down the stairs to the FAMILY ROOM. She focuses on a toddler sitting in a high chair with a sausage in his hand.

JESSIE (CONTINUED)

Hello, Max-y! How's my sweet pea?

(gives him a kiss and he giggles)

This is my darling baby brother, Max. Isn't he cute? Well, he looks cute, but he can be a terror, especially when I'm babysitting. You should see his tantrums – they're explosive! Mum, what's for breakfast? I'm famished!

JESSIE'S MUM

(out of shot)

I made some pancakes and sausages that are in the oven . . . the rest is up to you!

JESSIE helps herself and waves a
sausage at the camera.

JESSIE

Yum, thanks, Mum. Mmm, I love sausages! I
have a humongous appetite, maybe because I'm so active with
gymnastics and sports. People are always telling me to stop
jiggling and to sit still!

JESSIE (CONTINUED)

So over there on the sofa is one of my other brothers – Jake –
who's eleven.

Camera pans to boy intently playing a computer game.

JESSIE (CONTINUED)

Whatcha playing, Jake?
Minecraft? JAKE!
Hey, earth to Jake!

JAKE

Actually it's *Super Mario Kart*. Wanna play?

JESSIE

Yes! I'll wipe the floor with you!

(turns camera to film herself)

I'm ace at computer games, probably cos I spend so much time playing them with my brothers. There's Leon too, who's still in bed – he's sixteen. Gaming is one of the few things that helps me to keep still!

JAKE

Prepare to be annihilated!

JESSIE

(waving)

Time to end this vlog . . . bye, guys! Thumbs-up if you enjoyed the video and let me know what your favourite games are in the comments below. See you soon!

FADE OUT.

Views: 432

Subscribers: 523

Comments:

PrankingsteinCharlie: *Grand Theft Auto* all the way!!

lucylocket: New room looks fab! Love those zebras!

Carlydoesthesplits: Can you do a gymnastics challenge sometime?

gamegirl2000: I love *Sims* . . . just got the pet extension.

Jakethechamp: *Minecraft, Minecraft, Minecraft*!

HashtagHermione: Amazing editing Jess xx

(scroll down to see 74 more comments)

Chapter Eight

'And . . . that's a wrap! shouted Ms Kusama, applauding enthusiastically. 'Well done, all of you. We've practically got this in the bag. You should be really proud of yourselves. Take a break, then we'll go over the last scene one more time.'

It was Saturday morning and the *Grease* cast had had their first full-length run-through, with not-entirely-awful results. For Abby it had been a welcome distraction from her upsetting week and she'd had no problem remembering her lines and dance steps. In fact, she felt like doing it all over again! Performing live gave her an even bigger high than when she was vlogging.

And, unless it was her imagination, her hair was looking significantly less purple too now that it had been washed a few times. Blonde with a hint of mauve – that wasn't so bad.

'Dakota, sweetie, can you come over here?' called Maxine as the cast dispersed to get drinks or run to the bathroom. 'I need to charge my phone – can I borrow your charger?'

Dakota was at her side in seconds. 'Of course, Max! Oh, but I think we've got different phones.'

'Well, can you find me the right kind? I'm so stressed right now, and I need to think about Ms Kusama's notes before we start again,' said Maxine, fanning her face. 'I'm still not getting the delivery right on Sandy's final line. But also I really, *really* need to call my boyfriend and check my Twitter.'

'Say no more, Max – leave it with me!' As a thrilled Dakota rushed out of the room, her glossy hair swishing about, Abby and Lucy let out a snort.

'Earlier she had her running off to find her a Diet

Coke because Coke Zero wasn't good enough,' said Abby. 'Maxine is so bossy and annoying – she's basically Dakota squared!'

'Which is why Dakota adores her!' laughed Lucy. 'Anyway, you d-did really well today, Abs. I was watching you in the hand-jive scene and you're the best one out of all of us.'

'Plus, her hair is only *faintly* purple now,' said Charlie, who'd just come down from the lighting box. He stretched and gazed critically at Abby like an artist sizing up his own painting. 'Now that we're not being blinded by violet we can focus on the other elements of her performance.'

'Whoa, Charlie, I totally forgot you were up there!' gasped Abby. 'Were you watching the whole time?'

Charlie crossed his arms and feigned annoyance. 'Not just watching – working! Good to know you noticed my excellent lighting skills.'

Abby giggled. 'Aww, diddums, I'm sorry. I was too busy concentrating on not messing up my lines.' She waggled her eyebrows at him. 'Anyway, are you still on for our little . . . hashtag *project* . . . tomorrow?'

Lucy's eyes widened. 'Your *what*?'

Charlie opened his mouth to explain, but Abby clapped her hand over it. 'No telling! We don't want to ruin the surprise for everyone.' As Charlie gently removed her hand, she had the weirdest feeling that she wanted him to keep holding it. She dropped it abruptly. *Is he blushing?*

'Of course we're still on,' he said with a little smile. 'Bright and early start, don't forget. Right, back to the lighting box I go – a techie's work is never done. See you later, ladies!'

'That was . . . mysterious,' said Lucy once he'd gone. 'Aren't you going to give me even a s-single hint?'

'Nope!' Abby beamed. 'All will be revealed, soon enough!'

'Aw, Abbylicious, please t-tell me!' said Lucy. 'I'll love you forever?'

'No can do!' sang Abby. 'Just you wait. Ooh, there's

Ben – I wondered where he'd gone. Just going over to say hi.'

11.32

Lucy: Argh! At rehearsal and I still haven't told A about D&B. Don't wanna ruin her good mood. And . . . maybe we're wrong? Still no actual KISSING or anything?? xx

11.35

Jessie: True. I've got a bad feeling, though.

11.36

Hermione: Me too. Seeing Abby later for our study session, I won't mention it. X

Abby arrived at Hermione's house in a slightly distracted mood. She hadn't had the chance to talk to Ben for long at rehearsal, and when she checked her phone at home she was disappointed that he hadn't texted. And now her mother had taken it away, which meant she wouldn't be able to check again until tomorrow. So annoying!

'Hey, Abs, come in,' said Hermione, opening the front door in her favourite yellow-checked shirt and jeans.

'Thanks!' Abby noticed Hermione looked a little paler than usual, and slightly downcast. 'You OK?'

A split second of a pause. 'Yeah. I'm fine. You want some tea?'

'Please!' Abby loved the fragrant jasmine tea that was permanently on tap at Hermione's house. It smelled wonderful – and drinking it always made her feel peaceful somehow.

'I'll bring it up – you go and get settled in my room. My parents are out,' said Hermione.

As Abby entered the room, she quickly put her 'forgive me' present on Hermione's desk, then nestled into one of the big squelchy beanbags on the floor. She looked around, feeling slightly overwhelmed by the stacks of books that lined two of the walls – there seemed to be even more than the last time she'd visited. She didn't think she could read this number of books in her lifetime even if she did nothing but read!

'Here you go,' said Hermione, coming into the room with a tray of tea and biscuits. 'Ooh, what's that?' She hastily put down the tray and went over to her desk, immediately clocking the Harry Potter notebook that Abby had propped up against the lamp. 'Oh my god – awesome! Did you get this for me?'

'No, it's mine,' said Abby. 'You know how much I love young wizards. And – stationery.'

Hermione looked confused, then embarrassed. 'Sorry – I just assumed, but . . . cool notebook anyway, Abs. Did you see he's holding his Nimbus 2001?'

Abby laughed. *I have the sweetest friends in the world.* 'No, I didn't see. And, OF COURSE it's for you, you enormous nerd! I was just messing with you.'

Hermione grinned widely. 'Thank you! I love it.'

'It's a thank you for helping me,' said Abby. 'And . . . er . . . an apology from me for copying from you in the biology test.' She gestured at the notebook. 'Harry is going to do a spell to make sure it never happens again.'

'Sounds good to me. And you're welcome.' Hermione smoothed the cover adoringly as she plumped herself down on another beanbag. 'It's the perfect present, really, Abs. I can never have too many notebooks.'

'You do love your stationery,' said Abby, sipping her tea. 'Almost as much as I like my make-up.'

'Well, it's important!' Hermione looked at her intently. 'I know if I don't have my books and pens and high-lighters and stuff all ready and organized at the start of the new term I'm not going to enjoy myself at all. And probably fail all my exams.'

Abby rolled her eyes. 'As if! That would never happen – you ace every paper you touch.' She sighed. 'And you're not the one who got banished to the Learning Centre. I'm ACTUALLY failing, and I don't think any stationery – even as nerdy as this – is going to help me.' Someone like Hermione would never understand how hard she had to work.

'Listen, Abs, you don't have to be so dramatic,' said Hermione. 'You got diagnosed with ADHD, you're going

to have to work harder, which I'm going to help you with, and that's all there is to it. It's not the end of the world.' She put down her tea and smiled awkwardly. 'Cookie? It's a new recipe I'm trying.'

'It's just so humiliating,' said Abby, ignoring the offer. 'It's bad enough the teachers thinking I'm stupid, let alone being shamed by the likes of Kayleigh Jenkins in public.'

'I bet it's really hard. But all I'm saying is, you shouldn't care what other people think.' Hermione held out a cookie, waiting for Abby to take it. 'Just get your head down and study as much as you can.'

'That's easy for you to say,' Abby muttered, sullenly accepting the cookie and taking a bite. 'People aren't saying anything bad about you. Perfect grades, the teachers love you, you're totally ace at baking –' she held up the cookie as proof – 'this is incredible by the way . . . Yeah, you've read more books than anyone I know, you're going to get straight A stars in your GCSEs . . . You're sorted, basically.' She realized that Hermione had gone quiet and was staring at the floor. 'Hey, it's a good thing!'

'My life isn't that perfect,' said Hermione, picking at a loose thread on her jeans. 'I was looking at Jessie's vlog.'

'Oh yeah – wasn't it awesome!' said Abby, remembering her friend's crazy, funny energy as she zoomed around the house. 'She did so well on her own. I bet she's going to get us loads of new subscribers.' She grabbed another cookie.

Hermione nodded. 'Yeah, it was great. She looked like she was having so much fun with her family and . . .' She gulped. 'It's not that way at my house.'

Abby looked at her in concern. 'What, because you don't have any siblings? But you have loads of cousins, right? Plus, having a big family's not all that anyway. Look at what having a brother does to you! I mean why would anyone –' As Abby gestured at her still-vaguely-purple hair she realized that Hermione's shoulders were shaking.

Oh no, she thought, *has something really bad happened?*

'H, what's wrong?' she said gently. 'You can tell me.'

Hermione wiped her eyes. She looked up at Abby. 'It's . . . look . . . I don't care about siblings, OK? We've always been great as a cosy little unit of three. But now – well – my parents are splitting up.'

Abby couldn't stop herself from gasping loudly. 'As in *properly* splitting up? Are you sure? Maybe they're just having a break.' Hermione's parents had always seemed so civilized with each other – she couldn't imagine them arguing about anything.

'No, it's for good,' sighed Hermione. 'In fact, they're getting an actual divorce. They told me yesterday. I never saw it coming. That's the problem with being too wrapped up in stupid books all the time.' She looked at the Harry Potter notebook. 'No offence, Harry.'

'But why?' asked Abby, shocked. She put down her cookie. 'Did something happen?'

Hermione shrugged. 'Apparently they've been "growing apart",' she said, doing the saddest air quotes

Abby had ever seen. 'Looking back I guess I can see the signs – not fighting, but Dad's been working late at the office a lot.' She sniffed. 'And Mum's been kind of – off – recently. They say it's for the best, and maybe it is for them, but my life is going to be so awful now.'

Abby shuffled over on to Hermione's beanbag and gave her a hug. They both giggled as they wobbled over on to the floor.

'I can totally relate. It's the worst feeling,' said Abby. 'I was only seven when my parents split up, but I can still remember how awful that day was, the day they told me my dad was going away for good. I'd just come back from my friend's birthday party and there was this beautiful pink glittery cupcake in my party bag, but I suddenly couldn't bring myself to eat it.'

'That's sad,' said Hermione ruefully, filling up their cups with tea. 'What a waste of a cupcake. As it happens, I can't *stop* eating. All morning, I've been like a crazed hummingbird on the search for my next sugar fix.'

Abby smiled. 'I don't blame you. It's really hard. But

you'll start to get over it, eventually.'

'It doesn't feel that way,' said Hermione glumly. 'It feels like my life is completely ruined. I wasn't going to tell anyone, but I guess I can't even pretend to be cheerful right now.'

'Well, I'm here for you!' said Abby. 'Like you said to me – don't worry what people think.' She pretended to scribble down a prescription. 'Dr Abby prescribes the following: being moody as much as you want, several times a day even, rereading ALL the Harry Potter books AND watching all the films, baking a lot more cookies – and, and – just trying not to be a hero, OK?' She felt sad for her friend, and guilty for assuming that she was the only one with problems.

Hermione smiled bravely. 'Thanks, Abby. You know, I think you're going to help me more than I'm going to help you.' Her tone became suddenly businesslike. 'But we've got MASSIVELY distracted, and I'm putting my tutor hat on now.' She stood up and rapped the desk with a ruler. 'Professor Hermione says *time to study*!'

To: amazingabby@abbys_world.com

From: TheRealRedVelvet100@gmail.com

Hi Abby,

Sorry it's taken me a little while to email you back. Things have been hectic with my new book coming out and Vlogmas to prepare for! But I wanted to check in and say hey, especially as it sounds like you were having a rough time at school. I hope things are looking brighter for you now – to me you seem like a girl with A LOT going for you.

I think I'll be in your neck of the woods the week after next – we could hook up and do a vlog together for the Girls Can Vlog channel? Only if you're up for it, of course.

Love,

Tiff xxx

To: TheRealRedVelvet100@gmail.com

From: amazingabby@abbys_world.com

OMGGGG this is amazingggg news! Of course I'm up for it!! Name a time! xxx

VLOG 8

FADE IN: ABBY'S KITCHEN – EARLY MORNING

ABBY and CHARLIE are standing by the sink.

ABBY

(stage whisper)

Morning, Charlie. Did you sleep OK? And, more importantly, is

Josh still asleep?

CHARLIE

Snoring like a pig! I barely got a wink of sleep. Anyway, here I am . . . at your service for the Big Revenge Prank!

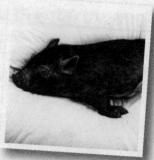

ABBY puts her hand over Charlie's mouth.

ABBY

Shhh, you'll wake him!

(to camera)

Hi, everybody! It's great to be back on the channel again. I had to take a little break because I got a bit behind in my schoolwork with everything going on in my life, but now I'm back. I really missed you guys! So today is a great day. My friend Charlie – who you'll know from the amazing Prankingstein – is going to help me play a revenge prank on my annoying brother, Josh, for dyeing my hair purple. It's faded now, but at the time . . . Well, you saw the video. I was not happy!

CHARLIE

And now IT'S PAYBACK TIME! Mwahahaha!

ABBY slaps CHARLIE playfully.

ABBY

Quiet! So it's five a.m. and Josh is still asleep in his bedroom,
which is upstairs at the end of the hall.

CHARLIE

And it's time for us to set up the best prank ever. I've been
wanting to try this one for ages! We considered a few options . . .
filling his room with balloons and hiding under them to leap out
and scare him . . . but that takes a lot of time . . .

ABBY

And balloons! Which we'd have to inflate – too much work.
We also thought about doing something really gross, smearing
chutney or brown sauce all over the loo seat so it looks like
poo . . . but I'd probably end up having to clean it up myself!

CHARLIE

So instead . . .

(whispers)

We are going to trap Josh in his bedroom by placing plastic cups
filled with water outside the door so he can't get out without
picking them all up or knocking them over! So let's get going . . .

ABBY

I've got more than five hundred plastic cups here, which we are
going to fill with water when they are in place outside the door.

CHARLIE films ABBY as she walks upstairs and down the hall to Josh's room with the cups and a jug of water. They both start putting out the cups, tightly side by side to cover the floor.

FADE TO BLACK.

FADE IN: ABBY'S HALLWAY – OUTSIDE JOSH'S ROOM
CAPTION: 20 MINUTES LATER

Pan of hallway filled with cups of water wall to wall for about three metres.

ABBY

(behind the camera)

Done! That was exhausting. I had to keep filling up the jug!

CHARLIE

The worst part was trying not to laugh and make noise.

Anyway, I think we're ready to rock and roll . . .

ABBY

Oh, I can't wait to see his face when he opens the door!

CHARLIE

(shouts)

Hey, Josh, man! You gotta get up!

ABBY

Wakey, wakey! Breakfast is ready downstairs, I've made pancakes.

JOSH

(from inside his room)

Ugh! Is it really time to get up? It seems really early . . .

CHARLIE

Come on, dude! We've got stuff to do today.

JOSH

OK, OK . . .

JOSH opens his bedroom door in
boxers and T-shirt and stands in the
doorway, facing the sea of cups
in front of him. He opens his
mouth in disbelief.

JOSH (CONTINUED)

What the—?

ABBY

Ha ha! Got you! This is payback for my hair . . . Good luck
trying to get out of there.

CHARLIE

(laughing)

You do look a bit stuck, mate.

(to Abby)

Look at his face!

JOSH

This is NOT FUNNY! I gotta pee really bad! How am I meant to

get to the toilet? What – you're filming this?

ABBY

'Fraid so! And don't go spilling water on Mum's new carpet . . .

she'll have a fit.

JOSH hops, trying to find a space to place his foot. He can't

see one.

JOSH

Am I supposed to pick up every single cup? ARGH! Charlie, you

little . . . did you help plan this? Where is the loyalty?

CHARLIE

(bent over, laughing)

Sorry, buddy! Too funny!

JOSH shuts his bedroom door.

FADE TO BLACK.

FADE IN: ABBY'S HALLWAY – OUTSIDE JOSH'S ROOM

CAPTION: 10 MINUTES LATER

JOSH opens door again.

JOSH

ARGH! I was hoping it was a bad dream . . . I need to go really

badly . . .

(crosses legs and hops up and down on the spot)

ABBY

Sorry, Joshy! You should have thought of that before

you pranked me! Anyway, get a move on. Breakfast is

getting cold.

CHARLIE

(from behind camera)

Yeah, come on! We've got lots of Prankingstein filming to do today . . .

JOSH

Argh! I hate you both!

JOSH lies down and starts trying to move the cups aside to make a clear path.

CHARLIE

Well, I'm ready for a pancake, how about you, Abs? We'll be back in ten minutes to see how you're getting on . . .

CUT TO: ABBY'S KITCHEN

ABBY

That was brilliant! Did you see his face? And it was hilarious when he was hopping up and down! Hope he can hold it long enough to get to the loo.

CHARLIE

Mate, it was classic!

ABBY

Thank you sooo much for helping me plan and carry out this

prank!

ABBY gives CHARLIE a kiss on the cheek.

ABBY (CONTINUED)

I couldn't have done it without you.

CHARLIE pretends to wipe it off.

CHARLIE

Any time! Now how about that pancake?

ABBY

It's coming! So, guys, I hope you guys enjoyed today's video. If so, give us a thumbs-up below. You could also suggest other prank ideas for the future! Oh, and I'm posting a link to Prankingstein so you can see Charlie in action on his own channel. By-eee!

CHARLIE and ABBY wave.

FADE OUT.

Views: 529 and counting

Subscribers: 633

Comments:

RedVelvet: Haha! So good to see you back, Abby

Amazing_Abby_xxx: I'm allowed back in 'small doses' – we'll see xx

lucylocket: LOL

jazzyjessie: You two make a great team! #CHABBY4LIFE

queen_dakota: Thought you were dead and buried . . . Did the special needs teacher let you back online?

billythekid: Totally insane!

PrankingsteinJosh: I'll get you back, both of you!

StalkerGurl: Wish I could have picked up the cups for you, Joshie xxx

(scroll down to view 45 more comments)

Chapter Nine

'He ended up spilling the water everywhere. I've never laughed so much,' Abby told the others on Wednesday at their lunchtime meeting. She was still on a high from the prank even though her mother had told her off in no uncertain terms when Josh had lost patience, knocking over the cups and almost ruining the new carpet.

Totally worth it, she thought with a grin.

'It was proper hilarious! That boy got what was coming to him,' said Jessie. 'So cheeky.' She pointed her knife at Lucy and Abby. 'And, speaking of cheeky, I can't believe you guys get the afternoon off today. I wanna miss double maths too.'

$$= \\ + \ 8 \\ ? \ 3$$

Abby smiled, excitedly swirling a strand of spaghetti with her fork. 'It's not like we're off shopping, Jess! It's the dress rehearsal!' Opening night was in three days' time and it was all the *Grease* cast could think about. For once Abby's mum and teachers had got off her back about her studies, realizing that she needed to give the performance her full attention.

'Today's our last ch-chance to get everything p-perfect,' said Lucy, nervously. 'Which is way more stressful than d-double maths!'

'Well, I know where I'd rather be,' said Hermione, looking horrified. 'Every time you talk about that show I feel more relieved that I didn't make the cut. Can you believe I even auditioned in the first place?'

Abby grinned at her. 'You did it for us; it was sweet! But you are going to come and watch on opening night, right? Maybe we can get you into the after-show party – if I'm not too busy with Ben, of course.' She noticed the others exchanging quick glances. 'What?'

'N-nothing,' said Lucy hastily.

'Of course I'll be there,' said Hermione. 'Um, I don't know if my parents can take me so I might need a lift.' She'd sworn Abby to secrecy about the divorce, which Abby understood. After all that had happened it was the least she could do.

'Let's go together,' said Jessie. 'I'll get my mum to take us. And we'll get seats near the front.'

'Guys, you're making me SO nervous,' said Lucy, putting down her fork. 'Wh-what if my stammer kicks in when I'm onstage?'

'Then you can take a deep breath and continue as normal,' said Abby, shovelling a last bite of spaghetti. 'It's going to be fine.' She noticed Dakota and Maxine leaving the canteen, Dakota stopping by the vending machine to load up on Diet Cokes for her idol. It was funny, she thought – in *Grease*, Rizzo was the one who pushed Sandy around, but in reality their roles were reversed. 'Come on, Luce,' she said. 'We've gotta run. Can't wait to finally try on my costume!'

*

Backstage, the cast was putting the finishing touches to their outfits. 'Oh no – well, that's awkward,' cackled Dakota in delight as she glanced over at Abby. In her dark Rizzo wig, tight black shirt and pencil skirt, Dakota looked older, more beautiful and more sophisticated than ever.

Abby rolled her eyes. 'Shut it, Dakota.' She gritted her teeth and yanked again at the zipper, but to no avail. *This can't be happening*, she thought frantically. Her fifties-style cigarette trousers were stuck fast, and the fly was gaping open. 'These obviously aren't mine – they're the wrong size.'

Ms Kusama came over from handing the boys their T-Bird jackets. 'They're definitely yours, Abby. Dakota passed me your measurements last week after Billie measured you. We had the others made earlier – yours were last minute.'

'Well, Billie must have measured me wrong, then,' said Abby, irritated. 'Not that there's much she can do about it now.' Billie, the sixth former who'd helped make the costumes, was off sick today.

Perfect.

'Pile on a few pounds, did we?' purred Ameeka, glistening in her satin Pink Ladies jacket. 'Dakota, Maxine's asking for you, babe.'

'*As if* I've put on that much weight! In a week!' Abby muttered angrily as they walked off. 'They're such idiots. Wait – did Ms Kusama say *Dakota* passed on the measurements . . . Oh my god!' Then Lucy came over in her Pink Ladies jacket and orange Frenchy wig, and Abby smiled despite her predicament. 'Ha! You look amazing, Luce!'

'Th-thanks!' said Lucy. 'I'm the only character who gets to have two wigs!' She held up a candyfloss-pink wig that she would wear in the scene where Frenchy accidentally dyed her hair the wrong colour. 'How's your – oh.' She noticed Abby's trousers as Ms Kusama rushed up with a couple of safety pins. 'You need some help?'

Their teacher, who was sweating profusely, looked gratefully at Lucy. 'Would you mind sorting her out?

These should do the trick for now. We can think up something better by Friday, so don't worry, Abby.'

Don't worry? Oh no, why would I worry? thought Abby. 'OK, so I'm going to pretend you're not pointing stabby sharp things at my crotch area!' she said as Lucy got to work in a quiet corner of the room. 'This is so humiliating, and I've got a hunch somehow Dakota is involved . . . She obviously wants me to look awful in front of Ben! Isn't it enough that I have to wear these stupid bunches in my hair?'

'Mmm-mmm,' said Lucy, her mouth full of safety pins.

Abby sighed, keeping her eyes on the room. 'Can you hurry up? It would be just my luck for Ben to walk in now. Although, what does it matter. He's going to see me in these massively unflattering trousers anyway.' She wondered fleetingly whether Red Velvet ever had to deal with this type of situation.

By the time they reached the dance-off scene an hour later, Abby's nerves had subsided, the music soared and she was completely lost in the moment. She and Eric danced breathlessly to the upbeat music, smiling crazily at each other as they tried to match its furious tempo. She glanced over at Ben, his cheeks flushed.

I'd never tell him, but he looks so cute with his gelled-back hair, and his—

RIIIIIIIP! The loud noise startled her out of her pleasant daydream and she looked around, bewildered. Eric had also heard it and he raised his eyebrows questioningly at Abby. She froze as she heard a gasp from the dancer behind her, and then realized what had happened. *Noooooooo!* Her too-tight trousers had split. Right across her bum!

As she struggled to remember what colour underwear she was wearing, she desperately tugged her shirt as low as it would go. It was no good. Ms Kusama down in the front row noticed what had happened and waved Abby offstage, not wanting to disrupt the flow of the performance. As Abby rushed into the wings, cheeks flaming, she glanced up at the lighting box – had Charlie seen? And what about Ben?

She didn't dare look in his direction. As she crept into the shadows, she heard Lucy stammering badly over her lines. Oh no! This was NOT how today was meant to pan out . . .

VLOG 9

Having a Bad Day? Lucy and Abby's Top Tips

8:25

FADE IN: ABBY'S BEDROOM

LUCY in cat-print PJs and ABBY in fleecy pink ones, on bed with
WEENIE. Tea lights on all the surfaces.

LUCY

So we're just going to w-wing it and see what happens . . .
r-right? I think this could be really good.

ABBY

(giggling)

OK, boss. If you say so!

LUCY and **ABBY**

(to camera)

Hi, guys!

ABBY

Today it's just Lucy and me and we're going to try something a bit different. We've both had a bit of a rough day and that got us thinking . . . Why don't we talk about bad moods and how to get out of them! I am definitely struggling today, though vlogging is helping already. So are my all-time favourite cosy PJs.

LUCY

Bad m-moods happen to everyone sometimes. It might be that there is a reason: you had a f-fight with your mom or best friend, you got a bad mark at school or it's your hormones . . . or you just messed up at something.

Book Report
book I learned th~
~ts of the char
salley. They
~ing ~

ABBY

Yeah. I'm normally a pretty positive person and usually feel happy but sometimes when I'm going through a lot I feel overwhelmed with stress and I just want to scream or cry. Today was one of those days – I won't go into why or blame anyone – but right now I just want to hide under the duvet with my sweetie Weenie who loves me unconditionally.

ABBY snatches up WEENIE.

ABBY (CONTINUED)
Don't you, Weenie Woo?

LUCY
Don't forget I love you too!
(laughing)

But you hiding under the c-covers wouldn't make a great video!

I understand how you feel . . . c-cos it happens to me as well.

(to camera)

And I'm sure all you guys have gone through this too. So the first

thing is to try to get things into p-perspective. It's one bad day, not

a bad life. It will p-pass and hopefully feel you'll better tomorrow.

ABBY

That's hard to believe right now! I still feel awful.

LUCY

My mom always says that the most important thing is to let it go . . .

'let it go, let it go' . . . as my little sister Maggie's favourite song goes.

Don't h-hold on to your anger or negative thoughts. You need to move

on, and the best way is to make a l-list of things you can do to make

yourself f-feel better.

ABBY

So, pampering or treating yourself is a good start. Chocolate always helps cheer me up!

LUCY

Yeah! And b-baking brownies or cookies and then sharing them with your friends is good. Baking is usually pretty c-calming, plus doing something k-kind for someone else always makes you feel better. What else?

ABBY

Having a long, hot soak in a bubble bath surrounded by scented candles and loads of Lush stuff always cheers me up. Ooh – and I have to have my favourite tunes playing.

LUCY

Definitely! For me, watching my f-favourite sad movie with loads of popcorn really helps. It never hurts to have a good cry. And how about s-something more active for when you can face going outdoors?

ABBY

(with a big grin)

Shopping? Shopping always cheers me up!

LUCY

Be serious, Abs!

ABBY

Well, I feel amazing after a long run . . . I guess it's those endorphins kicking in that boost your mood. But having a mad crazy dancing session and jumping around and singing along to some loud music can do the same thing. I just love dancing!

LUCY

Me too. And, s-sometimes, it's enough just going for a walk with your friend, having a hot chocolate and talking about fun, silly stuff. It can really lift your mood and r-remind you that you're not alone.

ABBY

So let's get dressed, take Weenie for a walk and grab a hot chocolate and a brownie!

(to camera)

OK, guys, well I hope this video wasn't too random . . . and
that it helps some of you who are also having a rough day.
Remember, sometimes it's good to talk about your feelings.

LUCY

Let us know if you l-liked this video by giving us a thumbs-up
and putting your own suggestions for b-banishing bad moods
down below!

FADE OUT

Views: 437

Subscribers: 704

Comments:

ShyGirl1: Going outside for fresh air ALWAYS makes me feel
awesome ☺

xxrainbowxx: You forget to mention pizza!!!

animallover101: If I had Weenie, I would never feel depressed.

girlscanvlogfan: Hope you're both feeling better soon. You rock xxx

HashtagHermione: Baking is always the best remedy!

dakota_queen: Ever tried walking in traffic?

(scroll down to see 42 more comments)

Chapter Ten

'I'm sure she doesn't *hate* you, Abby. Why would she?' Mrs Pinkerton said as she dropped off Abby in the school car park early on Thursday morning. Ms Kusama had scheduled an emergency last-minute rehearsal one day before opening night. Because of Dakota's stupid antics with Abby's costume yesterday, and an embarrassing stammering episode by Lucy, whose nerves had kicked in once she'd noticed her friend's humiliation, the dress rehearsal had spiralled into chaos and so they were having to do it all again.

'Mum, you're not listening to me.' Abby scowled. She felt exhausted and fed up. 'Dakota's been trying to sabotage me all along – obviously she's threatened by me or something, or she's just a weird and unhappy person – but, whatever her reason, it's driving me crazy! I never know what's coming next!'

Her mum gave her a sympathetic look. 'Well, chin up, sweetheart. Don't let her ruin your fun. This is going to be your week of stardom!'

But as her mum drove off and Abby walked towards the building her blood was still boiling. She was exhausted and she probably looked like rubbish. She'd been up half the night editing her collab vlog with Lucy and once she got to bed she'd hardly slept, worrying about what trick Dakota might pull on her today.

So much for de-stressing! she thought. *I need one of those Lush baths, like, yesterday!*

Abby tried to follow her own advice and think positive, but as soon as she entered the theatre and saw Dakota innocently swigging from a Styrofoam coffee cup onstage, she saw red.

'So, Dakota, what have you got in store for me today,

huh?' she challenged, pushing aside the other cast members and grabbing Dakota's shoulder. Ben gave her a startled look, but she was past caring.

'Whoa – easy there, girl,' said Maxine, stepping back. 'You nearly made me spill my coffee.'

Abby ignored her and continued to glare accusingly at Dakota.

'Morning, Abs,' said Lucy anxiously, walking over to her with a Tupperware box in her hand. 'C-come and try one of these muffins my mom made. Triple-choc – they're so good!'

'I wouldn't recommend it,' drawled Dakota. 'All those calories . . . we don't want another exploding trousers "wardrobe malfunction" happening today!'

Ben glanced at her in horror. 'Not cool, Dakota.'

Dakota flinched, visibly surprised at being told off. 'Whatever, Benjamin. I'm just saying, if Amazing Abby here hadn't been so amazingly greedy lately –' Abby gasped – 'and if Lucy Lockjaw had remembered how to s-s-speak yesterday, we wouldn't have needed this stupid extra rehearsal in the first place, and we could all have had a bit longer in bed this morning.'

The room went quiet as her words sank in, and Lucy's cheeks turned pink. Abby could tell that her friend wanted to defend herself but was staying quiet, worried that she might stammer. Where was Ms Kusama?

'Not that I'm the one who needs beauty sleep, by the look of it,' continued Dakota.

It's true – she looks as annoyingly fresh-faced as ever, fumed Abby. *No guilt keeping her awake at night, that's for sure*.

'Abby – do you want to borrow my under-eye concealer for those bags?'

There was a collective gasp from the assembled crowd. Ben shook his head and, while Ameeka giggled loyally, Abby couldn't help but notice that she looked uncomfortable too, her laugh tailing off awkwardly into the silence.

How DARE she, thought Abby.

'What?' said Dakota innocently. 'I'm only saying . . .

Dumb and D-D-D-Dumber over here have basically screwed up our show and now they show up to rehearsal looking rough.'

'Right, that's it!' shrieked Abby, knocking Dakota's coffee out of her hand and grabbing her long, sleek ponytail and giving it a yank. It felt so good! 'You think you're so funny and superior, but throughout this process you and your friends have tripped me up, given me the wrong rehearsal time, locked me in a toilet, messed up my costume – and NOW you're calling me ugly and picking on my best friend.' She yanked the glossy hair again, her face going bright red.

'Get off me!' screamed Dakota and gave Abby a big push. 'Ben! Get her off!'

Ben just shrugged. 'Sorry, but you kinda asked for it. Abby's right – you've made this whole thing really difficult for her, and I for one have no idea why.' He cleared his throat. 'It's not nice to watch.'

Dakota looked at him in shock. 'Seriously? You're taking her side? Ow!' Abby had aimed a kick at her leg.

'That's so going to bruise! You little cow!'

'He's not your boyfriend, you deluded freak,' said Abby. She could see Lucy looking at her in shock and she knew she was going too far, but she couldn't help herself.

'Guys, just cool it,' said Maxine in a bored voice, moving away from the commotion. 'I suppose this is what we get for involving Year Nines. I told Ms Kusuma it was a bad idea.'

'Max, it's not me that's the child, it's HER,' said Dakota. 'GET LOST!' she screamed at Abby, flinging her forcefully across the stage.

The atmosphere was tense as Abby stumbled and everyone watched to see what she'd do next.

She straightened up slowly, her head pounding. 'So? Are you going to apologize?' she said to Dakota.

'Come on, Abs, let's go and get a drink,' said Ben gently, putting his arm round her shoulder.

Still fuming, Abby glanced at him. 'Not now, Ben,' she snapped. 'Dakota, I'm waiting. Do you even *know* the word sorry?'

Dakota raised an eyebrow. 'I'm not apologizing for anything, loser. I *knew* it would be a disaster having you and Lucy in the show, and I've been proved right,' she said curtly, running a hand over her dishevelled hair. 'Ameeka, get me my hairbrush!'

Her hairbrush? Really? thought Abby.

'Where would you be without your slaves, eh, Dakota?' she called with a bitter laugh as Ameeka scurried over to Dakota's enormous fake designer handbag. 'When we leave school and we're in the real world you're going to get a shock – adults don't behave like this.'

'Thanks for the advice – did you pick that up in the Learning Centre?' Dakota smirked. 'Whatever . . . I'm going to get ready. Just be sure to keep your manky paws off me in future – or you'll regret it.'

A few people laughed as she stomped off backstage, Ameeka trailing behind her.

'Wow, Abby. She really had that coming,' said Eric, Abby's dance partner. She smiled at him uncertainly, trying to take comfort from his words. 'She's put you through hell, but I've never seen anyone stand up to her before.'

'Not sure if hair-pulling is the classiest way you could have dealt with it, though, Abby,' said Maxine disapprovingly. 'Good thing Ms Kusama missed that little scene. She'd definitely have chucked the pair of you off the show! You'd better hope she doesn't find out about it.'

Abby froze as she thought through the implications of what she'd done. Maxine was right – she'd put her beloved performance in jeopardy. And – worse – people got expelled for fighting!

'Well, I'm n-not surprised that Abby lost her temper,' said Lucy, finally finding her voice. 'I hate fighting, but D-Dakota can't get away with treating people like that. I'm already n-nervous about opening night and she knows she's making it w-worse. Oh, hey, guys.'

Charlie had arrived with the sound engineer and the props girl. 'Hi! Er, what's going on?' he asked, putting his bag down and looking around. 'There's kind of . . . a weird atmosphere in here?'

'Just the usual Dakota melodrama,' said Abby, suddenly uncomfortable and desperate to get off the subject. 'All sorted now, so let's get on with the show.'

'But . . . are you OK?' asked Charlie, noticing Abby's flushed cheeks and breathlessness. 'I saw your bad-mood vlog this morning, but it looks like you guys are still having a stressful time.'

Lucy glanced at him. 'Dakota's been extra-vile, and Abby l-laid into her big time. It was pretty intense.'

'I'm fine,' said Abby cheerfully. Not wanting him to worry, she grabbed his Nike baseball cap and put it on her own head. 'I styled it out with true Amazing Abbyness!'

'That's my girl,' grinned Charlie, snatching back the cap.

Ben was watching them from the other side of the stage. 'Yeah, Dakota was a cow and Abby was right to put a stop to it,' he called. 'But here comes Ms Kusama, so let's stop talking about it and get on with the show.'

'Exactly,' said Abby gratefully. 'Everyone listen to Ben!'

The sooner we can all forget about this, the better, she thought, as she took her place for the opening scene.

17.20

Abby: How cute was Ben this morning!

17.21

Lucy: I know – he definitely took your side against she who shall not be named!

17.22

Abby: First time he's ever done that.

17.23

Lucy: Plus he was jealous of u + Charlie.

17.24

Abby: Really? He did text me afterwards ☺

17.24

Lucy: You see? Totally jealous.

17.25

Abby: Bodes well for the cast party 🙂

17.26

Lucy: Exciting . . . but we need to get through the show first. Eek!!

17.26

Abby: We're going to ROCK IT xxx

VLOG 10

FADE IN: HERMIONE'S BEDROOM

There's a big Harry Potter film poster on the wall and bookshelves packed with books. JESSIE and HERMIONE are in jeans and hoodies on the beanbags.

HERMIONE

Hi, guys! So today Jessie and I are filming alone, as the others are busy with the final rehearsals for *Grease*. So glad I'm not involved in that as I would be paralysed with fear!

JESSIE

I know, and who's got time to learn all those lines, right?
They're doing great though and we're sooooo proud of
them. Anyway, today we're gonna play a game that loads of
YouTubers have been playing lately – it's called *Never Have I
Ever* or, wait, is it *Never Have I Never?*

HERMIONE

(laughing)

It's *Never Have I Ever*, you fool!

JESSIE

Ha ha, whatever! So you guys sent
in some questions via Snapchat
and we have to answer them
honestly with either
'I Have' or 'Never'.
Hermione, got the signs ready?

HERMIONE shows the signs to the camera.

JESSIE (CONTINUED)

OK, here goes . . .

HERMIONE

Never have I ever . . . been suspended from school.

HERMIONE holds up 'Never', JESSIE dithers . . .

HERMIONE (CONTINUED)

(shrieks)

You have!

JESSIE

No, but I once had so many detentions in the same term

I *almost* got suspended . . . Luckily the holidays came

just in time.

JESSIE holds up 'Never'.

JESSIE (CONTINUED)

My turn. Never have I ever . . . got caught passing a

note in class.

JESSIE lifts up 'I Have'. HERMIONE looks a bit uncomfortable and

also lifts up 'I Have'.

JESSIE (CONTINUED)

Really? You're bad!

HERMIONE

(seriously)

It was really important – I needed to

let someone know that their pen was

leaking ink on to the desk and their uniform.

JESSIE

Aw, you're adorable! OK, your turn.

HERMIONE

Never have I ever used
someone else's toothbrush
without telling . . .

HERMIONE immediately
lifts up 'Never'.

HERMIONE (CONTINUED)

Gross!

JESSIE

(shrugging)

Sure, lots of times at sleepovers when I've forgotten mine.

HERMIONE

Not mine, I hope! Ew! The germs! Your turn.

JESSIE

Never have I ever eaten a whole huge tub of ice cream by myself at one sitting.

JESSIE holds up 'I Have'.

JESSIE (CONTINUED)

Did it last week – toffee swirl and it was *dee-licious*! In my house, if you don't eat it straight away, someone else will snaffle it before you know it.

HERMIONE holds up 'Never'.

HERMIONE

No way! I'd be so ill. OK, so here's an embarrassing one. Never have I ever . . . kissed someone in a dream.

JESSIE

Everyone has, surely!

JESSIE holds up 'I Have'.

JESSIE (CONTINUED)

There was this boy last summer . . . anyway, at least I don't have to say his name! What about you, Hermione? Anyone apart from Daniel Radcliffe?

HERMIONE slaps JESSIE with her notebook.

HERMIONE

Don't be mean! I fancy people in real life too, you know.

HERMIONE holds up 'I Have'.

HERMIONE (CONTINUED)

And that's all you need to know! No way am I revealing any

secrets here.

JESSIE

OK, moving on . . . Never have I ever seen a ghost . . . If we're

talking real ghosts, not like at Halloween . . .

JESSIE holds up 'Never'.

JESSIE (CONTINUED)

I don't believe in any of that stuff. How 'bout you?

HERMIONE slowly holds up 'I Have'.

HERMIONE

So you might think this is weird, but I've seen my great-grandmother's ghost in the garden by the family shrine at my grandmother's house.

JESSIE stares at her, wide-eyed.

HERMIONE (CONTINUED)

It wasn't scary, though. She was just . . . there.

(awkward pause)

OK, changing the mood . . . Never have I ever gone skinny-dipping! Jess?

JESSIE

I love skinny-dipping!

JESSIE holds up 'I Have'.

JESSIE (CONTINUED)

We did it at night in the pool when we went to the

Caribbean . . . it was sooo fun . . . but I'd be too scared to do it in the ocean! Imagine those fish looking at you naked?

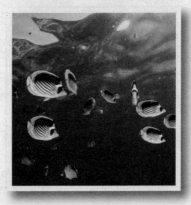

Hermione holds up 'Never'.

HERMIONE

I always swim in pools full of people . . . Anyway, I love my bikinis.

JESSIE

It's really fun! I promise, you'd love it. OK, last one . . . Never have I ever pretended to be someone else over the phone.

JESSIE holds up 'I Have'.

JESSIE (CONTINUED)

My brother asked me to pretend to be my mother and call in sick for him at school once . . . but I don't think they believed it!

(Hermione laughs)

I bet you've never done it.

HERMIONE toys with the 'Never' card before holding up 'I Have'.

HERMIONE

Well . . . this is embarrassing, but I might as well confess. Once I pretended to be from J. K. Rowling's agent's office to try to speak to her when she was staying in a hotel, but I got rumbled pretty quickly. They asked me for a password so I hung up. I probably would have been tongue-tied if I'd got through!

JESSIE

You are such a dark horse sometimes – I love it.

(they giggle)

OK, guys, so thanks for listening to us share some of our secrets. Give us a thumbs-up if you enjoyed it and don't forget to subscribe to our channel! Bye-ee!

HERMIONE and JESSIE wave.

FADE OUT.

Views: 412

Subscribers: 759

Comments:

girlscanvlogfan: You two are friendship goals!

funnyinternetperson54: The toothbrush thing is totally fine

StephSaysHi: No it's not – gross!

billythekid: We must be told, who did Hermione snog in her dream???

xxrainbowxx: Cute video

sammylovesbooks: I wonder what JK's password was?

(scroll down for 32 more comments)

Chapter Eleven

'I just peeked through the curtain and the theatre is already f-filling up,' said Lucy restlessly, pacing around backstage where the air was fizzing with nervous excitement. 'Hermione and Jessie are r-right at the front. And there are s-so many people! Like, hundreds!'

'That's a good thing!' replied Abby, posing and sticking her tongue out as Ben took a picture of her goofy Jan bunches, complete with pink ribbons. She couldn't wait to get started. 'And it's not that many compared to the number of people who are watching the channel.'

'I know, but we have editing and c-control when we're vlog—'

Lucy was interrupted by Ms Kusama coming backstage. 'Attention, please! Has anyone seen Ameeka?' she asked anxiously.

'No, but can I just say your outfit is totally on fleek, Miss Kusama!' cried Abby, impressed. Their teacher was wearing a black catsuit with sky-high heels and a hot pink belt cinching her waist.

'Well, thank you, Abby, that's kind of you to say.' Ms Kusama smiled at Abby, turning to look at her reflection in one of the backstage mirrors. 'You see, I wanted to look the part on your opening night, and at first I thought heels would be over the top, but then I thought, why on earth not, it's not every day that you launch a fantastic all-singing all-dancing production of everyone's favourite musical!' She gazed proudly at her reflection as the assembled cast waited for her to continue. 'Wait – er – where was I? . . . Oh yes! Ameeka? Her whereabouts? Anyone? Curtain's up in ten minutes!'

'She's here,' said Dakota, sounding annoyed as she spotted Ameeka coming up behind Ms Kusama. 'Finally!'

The tall, serious girl looked sweaty and uncomfortable. She pushed through the crowd and grabbed Dakota's arm before dragging her off into the corridor.

Unaware that everyone could still hear her, she whispered urgently, 'I can't do this, D. I feel sick!'

Abby felt an unexpected twinge of pity.

'Oh, for god's sake, you'll be fine,' Dakota could be heard snapping. 'Get it together. You haven't even done your make-up yet.'

They heard heavy breathing. 'I think . . . I have to drop out!' panted Ameeka. 'Every time I think about the curtain opening, I feel like I'm going to faint!'

Ms Kusama hushed the giggles that were breaking out backstage, then dashed out to talk to the panicking girl with impressive speed considering the height of her heels.

'Poor Ameeka,' said Abby to Lucy. 'I really feel for her. Now she knows what we went through the other day!'

Lucy nodded. 'I'm surprised, though. She's always seemed so c-composed.'

'You probably don't have a choice if you're in Dakota's all-star gang,' muttered Eric. 'Maybe Ameeka's been feeling nervous for weeks, and just hasn't been allowed to say it.'

As the rest of the crew made their final preparations, Ms Kusama guided Ameeka to get into costume and gently helped her through her hair and make-up, whispering reassurances to her as she went, with Dakota standing to one side and rolling her eyes. Abby watched nervously – she was relieved that the spotlight wasn't on her for once, but how would they cope with no Marty in the Pink Ladies? There was no understudy.

'Right, everyone, everything's under control. Ameeka's feeling better now,' announced the teacher eventually, as Ameeka sipped from a water bottle, her expression unreadable. 'Are we all ready? Danny? Sandy? OK – let's do this!'

'A wop-baba-lu-bop! A wop-bam-boom!'

The applause was deafening, and as the cast took

their bows Abby was on top of the world, her heart beating fast from the final high-speed dance routine.

Woohoo! We did it! she thought, relieved she'd remembered all her lines and dance steps. Her confident depiction of the funny, junk-food-eating Jan had people roaring with laughter. There had been a couple of awkward moments where Ameeka had forgotten her lines, but apart from that the show had been a huge success – and Lucy's stammer had barely surfaced at all.

Abby high-fived her friend as the Pink Ladies got their own special curtain call, smiling at Ameeka too. 'Well done,' she whispered. 'We did it!'

'Are you telling me you didn't hear her mess up her lines, like, five different times?' hissed Dakota.

'Oh, Dakota. Shut up!' said Abby cheerfully. Nothing could dampen her mood. 'Come on, Luce, and you, Ameeka – there's a cast party with our names on it!'

After a quick hello to their families and friends ('You guys are both my absolute heroes,' said Hermione earnestly, 'almost as talented as Emma Watson!') the girls got changed and then made their way to the school hall, which had been decked out with food, drinks and some iPod decks and speakers which were already blaring out music.

'Look, there's Charlie!' cried Abby. 'How did he get down from the lighting box already?' He was on a ladder attempting to attach a disco ball to the ceiling. *Always Mr Practical,* she thought fondly. A pink-and-black banner against one of the walls proclaimed 'WELL DONE, TEAM GREASE!'

'Great job, guys!' said Charlie, carefully stepping down the ladder. 'Now we have to do it all over again!'

'Same to you,' said Abby, giving him a high-five. 'Well-lit, my friend! And yeah – roll on tomorrow.'

'Can we please not think about the n-next few nights,' begged Lucy. 'I'm j-just relieved we got through this one.'

Abby squealed as someone tugged her hair. 'Yo, Jan, keeping the bunches in?'

'Yes, for now.' She grinned, turning round to face Ben, barely noticing as Charlie and Lucy wandered off. She'd done her make-up more naturally after the show, but she knew that the Jan bunches were cute on her. And she could see Ben's warm eyes twinkling at her, even if he did look slightly ridiculous still wearing his T-Birds leather jacket.

Just play it cool for a bit, she told herself. 'Nice job, Kenickie,' she said breezily. 'See you on the dance floor.' He gave her a wink and she headed for the snack table, walking on air.

Her good mood and sense of anticipation came to an abrupt end, however, when Dakota and Maxine entered the room twenty minutes later.

She looks . . . Photoshopped! was Abby's first thought.

Dakota was show-stoppingly stunning, even by her own standards. Her glossy hair had been curled to perfection, and she was wearing a tight red dress and killer black sandals. Air-kissing Maxine, she strode gracefully over to the group of T-Birds, emitting her vanilla scent as she went, aware that all eyes were on her.

'Er . . . did anyone t-tell her this was a party in the school hall?' giggled Lucy. 'Bit much, isn't it? It would be a shame if she dropped some Wotsits or Ribena down that dress – it l-looks designer!'

'That girl is ridiculous,' said Charlie, emptying a bowl of crisps into his mouth. 'She's so self-obsessed it's pathetic. And soooo boring! Come on, let's hit the dance floor. I might get my camera out! Abby, you coming?'

But Abby ignored him, still transfixed by Dakota, who was now talking to Ben. 'She's been planning this for weeks,' whispered Ameeka. 'And she decided to upgrade the dress when Ben lost his temper with her at the dress rehearsal.'

Abby's cheeks burned, and she quickly pulled her bunches out. 'Does she – does she think she has a chance with him?'

Ameeka looked at her pityingly, a trace of her bitchy side reappearing. 'Babe, it's the only reason she wanted to join the musical. She's been after him for ages. He's obviously up for it too.'

As Abby looked over again she felt her stomach fall into her shoes (a pair of glittery Converse – what *had* she been thinking when she chose those to wear – was she *five*?). Dakota had put her arm round Ben and he was laughing into her beautifully made-up face.

'I thought he hated her – he said she was lame! And he was flirting with me earlier,' whispered Abby. 'Didn't you see?'

'Whatever,' said Lucy, sensing trouble. 'Charlie's r-right – let's have a dance. Loads of people are dancing now, even Ms Kusama. Look!'

They all laughed at the sight of their teacher shaking it off to Taylor Swift, throwing her hair around with wild abandon . . . and headed off to join her on the dance floor. Apart from Abby, who kept staring at Ben and Dakota . . . even as he cupped his hand behind her glossy head, still laughing at whatever she was saying, and drew her towards him into a kiss . . .

VLOG 11

FADE IN: ABBY'S BEDROOM – NIGHT

ABBY still in jeans and black top from the party, with messy hair and panda eyes. The room behind her is messy, and discarded outfits are piled on the bed.

ABBY

Hey, guys. It's really late and I have to be quiet as my mum thinks I'm asleep. I just got back from the *Grease* first-night cast party and it's my turn to vlog. Originally, I grabbed this slot cos I thought it would be a really upbeat celebration of an amazing evening . . . but what can I say? That balloon got well and truly burst tonight. So I'm going to do something totally unscripted and uncool and just open my heart to you guys and tell you how I feel . . .

ABBY wipes her eyes and takes a deep breath.

ABBY (CONTINUED)
So here goes . . .

It's been a really tough term for me with all the hard work I've had to put into *Grease* – learning the lines, which wasn't easy for me, learning the dance routines, which wasn't easy either, and fending off all the sabotage attempts and harassment from people who had it in for me – for no good reason except that they are mean. Jealous. Spineless. Cruel.

On top of that I've had lots of stress at school about my work and how to try to improve it. And I am trying really, *really* hard.

ABBY starts crying.

ABBY (CONTINUED)

The extra work means cutting down on treats and YouTube and, most importantly, time with my friends but I've tried really hard to be mature and more disciplined.

Through this difficult time I've had my loyal friends to support me, PLUS a hopeful star on the horizon. Something I really wished for and dreamed of and hoped would come true. But tonight that dream turned to ashes . . .

I don't know if I was the victim of a cruel plot or just completely self-deluded – or a bit of both – but tonight I was betrayed. And I feel like a complete fool. It really, REALLY hurts.

ABBY starts to sob heavily.

ABBY (CONTINUED)

I'm going to try and sleep now . . . but thanks for all your

support, guys. It means a lot to me. Goodnight.

ABBY sniffs and turns off camera.

Comments disabled.

Chapter Twelve

23:49

Lucy: I saw the video – are you OK?!!

00:03

Lucy: I'm so sorry that happened to you – Ben is the worst 😵

08.21

Lucy: Are you there? Pick up the phone xx

Abby scrolled through the messages and watched her screen flash as Lucy called again. She knew her friend was worried about her, but she just couldn't find the energy to pick up and talk to her – or even tap out a message. It was as if doing the vlog last night had completely drained her.

She'd woken up at five a.m. and taken it down, suddenly full of regrets and panic about making her embarrassment and anger so public, but Lucy – and probably loads of other people – had already seen it. Abby prayed that Ben hadn't, but then again – who cared? He'd been stringing her along the whole time.

How could he have let me down like that? she thought for the millionth time. Why had he texted her and flirted with her if all along he'd always wanted Dakota instead?

'Boys are scum, Weenie,' she said, munching handfuls of sugary cereal from the box she kept hidden in her room, then lay back on her bed leaning her head gently against Weenie's soft warm body. The normally hyperactive pug seemed to realize that she needed peace and quiet, and he lapped gently at her cheek with his rough little tongue, causing the first

smile of the day to creep over her face.

It was swiftly replaced with a frown as her phone pinged again. 'Luce, get the hint: I'm not in the mood to talk,' she muttered, glancing at the text. 'Give a girl a break!' But it was from an unknown number:

08:42

> **Unknown number:** Hey, Abby, is this still your number? It's Tiffany. I've been too busy to email. Sorry this is so last min but are you girls around this afternoon to film something Xmas-y together? I'll be in the area from 3. Let me know. Would love to meet up! xxx

Abby nearly choked on her cereal.

When Tiffany had stopped replying to her emails, she'd assumed she didn't have time to film together any more. She jumped to her feet, startling Weenie who started yapping and running round in circles.

'This is it, Weenie!' she cried, picking him up and kissing his face. 'This is my reward for having such a rubbish time recently. The day has come . . . We're actually going to vlog with the one, the only, the STUNNING, the AMAZING RedVelvet!'

She called the others excitedly one by one, Lucy first, brushing off their anxious questions about Ben (it turned out they had all seen her video). Breathlessly she told them the news about Tiffany, and they all agreed to drop everything and come round to Abby's house to prepare for the vlog. Thankfully her mum and brother were out Christmas shopping all day (she'd feigned a headache to get out of it), so they'd have the house to themselves.

'Did Tiffany say w-what she'd be wearing?' asked Lucy when Abby called her again ten minutes later to discuss outfits.

'Oh my gosh,' cried Abby, panicking. 'Tiffany! I never messaged her back to confirm!'

She could practically hear Lucy rolling her eyes at the other end of the phone. 'You're kidding me, right?'

'I'm doing it now – chat to you later!' shrieked Abby.

She ended the call and, fumbling through her messages, found the one from Tiffany and hastily typed out a reply:

09.11

> **Abby:** YES! All four of us are in!
> What do you need us to prepare? xx

The reply came seconds later.

09.12

> **Tiffany:** Awesome! ☺ 😄 So,
> any ideas for what we could film? xx

> **Abby:** AS IT HAPPENS, YES! LOADS!

When the doorbell rang ten minutes later, she dashed downstairs, phone still glued to her palm. Opening the door, she was surprised to see Charlie.

'Hey!' she said, giving him a huge hug. 'Wasn't expecting you!' He looked a bit startled, and she realized she was acting more cheerfully than the last time he'd seen her – at the party – and A LOT more cheerfully than in the video, if he'd seen that. Something about his expression made her think he probably had.

'So, how are you doing?' he asked, coming in and closing the front door. She noticed how red his cheeks and the tip of his nose were. 'Cold out there! Hey, Weenie.' The dog pattered up to him and started nibbling one of his shoelaces.

'I'm great – sorry if I was a disaster last night, but I'm feeling so much better today,' said Abby with a smile. 'Fancy a drink or anything? Josh is out with Mum. I can't be long, though.'

Charlie followed her through to the kitchen, shrugging off his parka. 'Oh right . . . we were meant to be filming today . . . Guess I forgot to remind him. That guy has got a memory like a sieve.' As he sat down at the table and looked up at Abby, she noticed that he didn't seem that disappointed that Josh was out. Or was she just imagining it?

'Coke, smoothie or coffee?' she asked, suddenly feeling a bit flustered.

'Coffee, please, as long as you chuck in four sugars,' he said, grinning as she pulled a disgusted face. 'What? I need the energy!'

'If you say so,' she giggled. *Am I blushing?* she thought, feeling her cheeks heat up. *Yes, I'm totally blushing. But why? – it's only Charlie!*

There was a pause and Abby put the radio on, Mariah Carey's 'All I Want for Christmas' suddenly blaring out across the kitchen.

'So, it's good to see that you're not letting that Ben idiot get you down,' said Charlie as she turned away to fill the kettle. 'I didn't want to say anything before because I could see you were friends, but he's an attention-seeking little loser. He's not worth your time – trust me.'

Abby flinched, the hurt and humiliation coming back in a flash. 'I wasn't really friends with him, I guess . . . It was just fun to do rehearsals together, and then it felt like things were getting more serious . . .' She turned round and Charlie was staring straight at her, an unusually earnest look on his face. 'But maybe that was just in my head! I sometimes let my imagination run away with me. It's no big deal.' *Please can we change the subject*, she pleaded silently.

'He definitely led you on, though, Abby . . . We all noticed it. I don't know what he was up to exactly, but it wasn't cool.' Charlie cleared his throat. 'Just remember that you're worth a million of him, OK? Any guy would be lucky to be with you.'

'Aww, excuse me while I vom into the sink!' she laughed. This was the first time they'd ever had such a serious discussion and his words were erasing the pain of last night like magic. Was he just being nice because she was Josh's sister?

She brought him his coffee and sat down next to him, humming along to Mariah. 'So anyway – what were you and Josh meant to be filming today?'

'Well, this music is kind of appropriate actually!' Charlie grinned. 'We were going to do this prank on members of the public involving this –' He whipped out a piece of mistletoe from his pocket. 'Phew, that's been stabbing me in the leg all morning! So, basically, we pretend we're doing a survey, and ask them a few questions about their Christmas plans. Then we ask them if they believe in the power of mistletoe while holding the mistletoe like this –' He held it up between his face and Abby's.

She laughed. 'What, and then you expect them to snog you?'

'Well, a peck on the cheek at least,' he said. He glanced at her, and the atmosphere shifted. 'I bet Amazing Abby would never fall for it, though.'

Abby froze. This was rapidly turning into the weirdest morning ever! 'I dunno, maybe?' she said giggling, as Charlie continued to look into her eyes and the music on the radio switched to 'Santa Baby.'

'Abby baby . . . just put a present under the tree, for me . . .' he sang softly.

Abby's heart started pounding. She didn't know whether to laugh or get nervous – he was so cute! Her phone beeped on the table and she glanced down. 'It's from Ben!'

Ben: We need to talk. Call me? xxx

'Er . . . let's ignore that,' said Charlie, switching it to silent.

'Good idea.' Abby grinned, looking at him, dangling the mistletoe with a glint in his eye. 'Now where were we? Oh yeah, you wanted to try out your stupid prank on me.'

She moved closer to him and before she knew it their lips had touched. *We're kissing!* she thought as the butterflies in her stomach went bonkers. *Still kissing! This is crazy! He smells amazing!*

DING-DONG! DING-DONG!

They pulled away as the doorbell rang repeatedly. 'That must be the girls – we've got some urgent Girls Can Vlog business to attend to,' said Abby, giggling hysterically. 'That was . . . fun!'

'Yeah, sure was,' said Charlie with a shy smile,

standing up and scratching the back of his neck. 'Not sure if I want to play the prank on anyone else now. See you soon?'

'Sure!' Abby sang, feeling on top of the world as she dashed for the door. 'See you soon, Charlie!'

VLOG 12

FADE IN: ABBY'S FAMILY ROOM – DAY

ABBY, LUCY, JESSIE and HERMIONE, wearing bright and glittery Christmas jumpers, are sitting on the sofa and beanbag chairs in ABBY'S family room. REDVELVET/TIFFANY is holding her bichon frise, BAMBI, wearing a Santa hat, and WEENIE is running around in an elf outfit.

ABBY

Hi, everybody! Today is a totally impromptu video because we have a fan-dabby-tabulous surprise appearance from the totally amazing RedVelvet – aka Tiffany! We are so excited!

HERMIONE

And honoured . . .

ABBY

Obviously that too . . . to have this HUGE YouTube star with us today to do a collab!

TIFFANY

(laughing)

OK, chill out, girls . . . It's really not that big of a deal. I just wanted to check in on my favourite new channel, Girls Can Vlog, and see how you're doing as well as wishing you a merry Christmas! I'm so thrilled to be here with you and to celebrate the success of your channel, which is almost at one thousand subscribers.

LUCY

It's s-so exciting!

TIFFANY

Anyway, I know that all kinds exciting things have been happening in your lives – like the *Grease* show. I remember that song, 'Summer Nights'!

ABBY

Hmmm, not so much loving as it turned out, but, yeah, we rocked it last night and we've got four more performances to go! It's been a challenge – on all kinds of fronts – but it's amazeballs – if I say so myself. And Lucy is so fantastic as Frenchy!

LUCY

Abs, you're embarrassing m-me . . .

JESSIE

You're both fab! And now for the questions! Over to you,
Hermione . . .

HERMIONE

Yeah, so we didn't have much time to prepare so we thought
we'd do our own Christmas Q and A Tag. We'll leave the
questions in the description box below so that you guys can
answer the questions in your own vlogs later!

TIFFANY

Whoo, better get started, then! Who's asking the questions?

HERMIONE

ME! So the first question is: What is your favourite Christmas
movie?

TIFFANY

Hmm. That's a tough one. Probably *Love Actually* or maybe *Home Alone*. Whoops – there goes Bambi, he wants to play with Weenie!

The dogs run around playing together.

JESSIE

My answer is definitely *Elf* ! So funny!

LUCY

I l-love that too but I also love *How the Grinch Stole Christmas*. Little Cindy Lou who reminds me of my little sister . . .

TIFFANY

Cute! How about you, Hermione?

HERMIONE

Well, I really love *The Snowman* – 'Walking in the Air' just makes me want to cry . . . sorry!

(coughs awkwardly)

So moving on. Next question is: What is your favourite

Christmas food?

JESSIE

Pigs in blankets! Yum!

TIFFANY

Gingerbread cookies. No contest.

ABBY

Mince pies with brandy butter. You love those too, don't you,

Weenie-Woo?

LUCY

Christmas pudding! They d-didn't have it in America.

HERMIONE

Next up, favourite Christmas song?

TIFFANY

Well, my favourite is a real oldie although it keeps getting covered . . .

(starts singing)

'Santa Baby – oh, I've forgotten the lyrics . . . dum de dum and

hurry down the chimney tonight!'

(giggles)

ABBY

Oh, I've heard that! It's so sassy! I love Mariah Carey's 'All I

Want for Christmas is You'!

LUCY

That's my f-fave too, but I also like 'Santa Claus is Coming to

Town' – the Justin Bieber version, obvs!

JESSIE

Ooh, I really like 'I Saw Mommy Kissing Santa Claus' because it reminds me of my mum and dad and all the wonderful Christmases we've had together!

HERMIONE

(impatiently)

OK, enough of that. Next question. What is on the top of your Christmas wish list?

TIFFANY

Donations to my favourite animal charities: one which protects elephant and rhinoceros hunted for their tusks and

(to Lucy)

also now to your city farm.

LUCY

Awesome! I would love a n-new phone – an iPhone – cos mine is a hand-me-down from my mom and pretty old. Abs, what about you?

ABBY

I'd really like studio lights to help me when filming.
Daylight can be very dark!

JESSIE

This question is hard . . . I'd like some cool new gymnastics kit,
but I guess what I really want most is my own skateboard so I
don't have to borrow my brother's. How about you, Hermione?

HERMIONE

Well, I've always got a long list of books that I'm dying to read,
but now that I find myself vlogging I could really use a good
camera for filming.

TIFFANY

I'm impressed – you're all so dedicated!

LUCY

It's just so much fun. I can h-hardly remember what it was like before we started the channel – can you, Abs?

ABBY

No . . . but now I think it's time to party: have some goodies to eat, turn up the Christmas music LOUD and get into the festive spirit!

JESSIE

WOOHOO! Merry Christmas, everyone!

MONTAGE: the girls laughing, eating cakes, decorating Abby's tree, wrapping presents, dancing with Tiffany and waving at the camera while the dogs run amok.

FADE OUT.

Views: 25,365

Subscribers: 4,789

Comments:

MagicMorgan: OMG GOALS

xxrainbowxx: Love this ♥

RedVelvetsuperfan: WOW WOW WOW

girlscanvlogfan: I would watch your channel without RedVelvet but she is hashtag *gorgeous*!!!

RedVelvet: Thank you for having me – SUCH a fun day xx

animallover101: Weenie + Bambi for life! 😌

ShyGirl1: Best video ever!!

HashtagHermione: Er, guys, we're nearly at 5K subscribers 😮

lucylocket: !!!!

Amazing_Abby_xxx: Merry Christmas, you guys! Love you loads xx

(scroll down for 390 more comments)

Top Ten Tips for Making Your Own YouTube Videos

Here are some tips for making your own YouTube videos, like Abby and the gang! Please be aware that to set up a YouTube account you must be at least thirteen. But you can still do some filming for fun if you're under thirteen – all that practice will come in handy when you are old enough to have your own channel and take the internet by storm.

1) ADVANCED LIGHTING

As we mentioned in the TOP TIPS section of *Lucy Locket: Online Disaster*, when starting out, most new vloggers just work with natural lighting. Once you are a more experienced YouTuber, you'll notice how much difference good lighting can make. Unless you live somewhere with constant sunshine – not the UK then! – you may need to add extra lighting when filming.

For a cheap option, adding table or floor lamps to the overhead lighting in your room can make all the difference. Alternatively, you can save up to buy some studio lights, which come at a variety of prices and can be ordered online. There are a few different types: soft box lights, umbrella-stand lights and ring lights, which are good for filming small things and close-ups.

TOP TIP: A lot of YouTubers have made videos talking about equipment, which will help you to research products before you buy!

TOP TIP: If you have more than one battery for your camera, make sure the spare is fully charged for when the other one runs out.

2) SHOOTING FIXED-CAMERA VLOGS

When recording a static video, try to make sure the camera is held in a fixed position, as handheld shots can be a bit wobbly. Before you start recording, ensure that everything you want in frame is included in the shot. Nothing can be more frustrating than recording a whole video, then realizing you've cut your head off! A friend can help make sure you're in frame and in focus or, if you're shooting alone, do a test run and check the playback before starting to film your full vlog.

TOP TIP: A tripod gives great stability and is very useful for sit-down videos.

3) SHOOTING ON-THE-GO VLOGS

If you are vlogging on the move, try to vary your shots to make the video visually interesting. Experiment with unusual angles, for example focusing on your feet while you are walking, or shooting upwards from a lying-down position.

TOP TIP: Always shoot in the highest resolution you can.

TOP TIP: For good audio quality, shoot as close as possible to the subject.

4) BASIC EDITING

This can be tricky when you first get started, but don't worry – your editing will improve with practice. As you get more experienced, you will want to be able to fix any glitches and improve the quality of your videos.

One thing to remember is that your videos should be balanced: there should be an intro, then the main body of content and finally an outro. Most beginners use iMovie or Windows Movie Maker for editing, which comes as standard on most Macs and PCs.

TOP TIP: If the video is shaky, try the stabilization effect or slow down the film.

TOP TIP: Boost the volume if your recording is too quiet, but be careful the sound doesn't distort.

5) ADVANCED EDITING

More experienced vloggers sometimes prefer to use more advanced editing programmes such as Final Cut Pro, Adobe Premiere or Sony Vegas, which are much more sophisticated and offer a wider range of effects and editing options. This software is very expensive, however, so saving up for it is a big commitment. In light of this, some experienced vloggers prefer to stick with standard editing software and spend their money on things that they can vlog about instead.

TOP TIP: Use colour correction to lighten dark videos, drop shadows and lift highlights.

TOP TIP: Try not to be a perfectionist! The content and mood of your video are more important than expert filming or editing.

6) BUILDING YOUR CHANNEL

Always remember that the whole point of vlogging is to make the videos that YOU (the maker) want to make and enjoy making. If you do this, you will connect with other like-minded people who will grow to like you and your vlogs and subscribe to your channel.

TOP TIP: Use social media like Twitter, Snapchat and Instagram to spread awareness of your channel.

7) GROWING YOUR AUDIENCE

Once you've started to gain some subscribers, you will be able to see which videos are most popular and start to engage with your viewers about new vlog ideas. The best way to build your audience is to make vlogs that people enjoy – although the number-one reason you should vlog about a subject is because YOU (the maker) want to. If you have fun, your viewers will too. So relax and enjoy yourself!

TOP TIP: When contacting fellow YouTubers, don't post comments asking for subscribers or for people to watch your videos. Be genuine and connect with people and videos you enjoy!

TOP TIP: Be safe! Never give out your address or phone number when contacting new people online.

8) TAG VIDEOS

If you enjoyed Abby and the gang's Christmas tag video at the end of this book, why not search YouTube for fun tags and make your own tag video? This is a really great way to connect with other vloggers. When you're done, mention your favourite YouTubers and send them a link. Maybe they'll do your tag too!

9) FILMING WITH PETS!

Do you have a cute dog like Weenie, or maybe a cheeky guinea pig? They could be fun to feature in your vlogs, but be prepared to let them steal the show! Also, you can be sure that any careful planning will go out of the window when you're filming with animals.

TOP TIP: Feature your pet in the intro to a video, for a short but sweet guest appearance!

10) WHEN IN DOUBT – WAIT!

Remember how Abby regretted uploading her emotional video from Chapter 11 and took it down a few hours later? If you're not sure about posting a video, there's probably a reason for that. Try asking yourself a few questions first:

* Do you want people to see this?
* Remember that once something goes on the

internet it is there forever. Even if you take the video down, someone else could have copied it or filmed it on their phone, and could repost it without your permission.

* If you aren't one hundred per cent sure or one hundred per cent proud of your video, don't post it.

And always remember . . . **STAY SAFE ONLINE!** Check with your friends and family that they are happy for videos in which they feature to be shared online BEFORE posting. And NEVER give away your identity, address or details of your school – so don't wear your school uniform when vlogging and don't film in your garden if it's easily recognizable.

Turn the page to read an extract from . . .

GIRLS CAN VLOG

Hashtag Hermione
Wipeout

Coming soon!

'You were right, Luce, this place IS like Downton Abbey,' said Morgan in wonder as the girls reached their form room. Morgan had been allowed to shadow Lucy for the first day of term before heading back to the US with her parents. 'Hermione, it's so great that you were here to show Lucy around when she started, it's *sooo* different to our school back home.'

Hermione smiled. That first term seemed like such a long time ago now. 'Lucy did great – apart from slipping in a giant puddle on her first day!'

'It *was* a pretty effective way of getting yourself noticed,' teased Jessie. 'By the entire class!'

'P-please don't remind me,' said Lucy, sitting down at her desk and sharing around some leftover Christmas cookies from a container she'd retrieved from her bag. 'And it wasn't just our class. Dakota's video f-footage meant that the whole school w-witnessed my humiliation.'

'Oh yes, that was so EVIL of her,' cried Morgan. 'Where is this famous Dakota anyway – I've got beef with her!'

She glanced around curiously, taking stock of the other teenagers. 'Also, Abby, where is that cute dude, Ben, the one you were in *Grease* with? Lucy told me all about it. He's in your class, right? Do you like him as much as Charlie?'

Abby froze – her face a picture of embarrassment, and Hermione cringed in sympathy. Morgan had such a loud voice and Ben was only a few metres away from Lucy's desk. He was doing a good job of pretending not to listen and looking at something on his phone, but Abby's face had started to go bright red. Like with Charlie, Hermione wasn't sure what was going on, but she knew that it was a sensitive topic – especially after Ben had snogged Dakota at the *Grease* after-party.

'So, *are* Ben and Dakota together now?' Morgan asked loudly. 'Abby, you are so awesome I refuse to believe he picked her over you!'

Hermione couldn't help but giggle as Abby, in sheer desperation, lunged at Morgan and stuffed a cookie in her mouth.

'Students of 9F, your attention please!' Miss Piercy called a few minutes later over the back-to-school chatter. Hermione looked up from showing Lucy one of her favourite Christmas presents, a Harry Potter water bottle complete with the Hogwarts crest. 'Welcome back – and hello, Morgan, nice to have you with us today.'

'Thanks, it's great to be here!' said Morgan cheerily. 'Love that top, by the way!'

She's so confident, marvelled Hermione to herself, I could never talk to a teacher like that, especially one I'd never met before. She caught Abby's eye and tried not to giggle.

'Well, thank you very much,' said the teacher, glancing down at her turquoise-and-white polka-dot shirt. 'Now class, I'm sensing a new-term restlessness amongst you. I too am sorry that Christmas is over and that we are all stuck back in this classroom, but there is some news which may just take the edge off . . .'

'Homework has been discontinued?' Jessie shouted out.

'Jamie Oliver is taking over our school dinners?' called a boy named Eric. Ben cheered loudly in support of the idea and Hermione saw Abby glance at him shyly.

'Nearly as good as both of those,' said Miss Piercy with a smile. 'A half-term ski trip to France for Year Nines! It's a lovely resort in the Alps that the school goes to every year. A wonderful opportunity for those of you who are interested – all abilities welcome, and we can even cater for snowboarding lessons if enough of you are keen. A sign-up sheet is going up on the noticeboard.'

A ski trip? thought Hermione, looking at Lucy, their faces slowly lighting up together. That actually *was* exciting!

'I c-can't wait! This is g-going to be intense,' whispered Lucy, her stammer more pronounced with all the excitement. 'I love skiing! We should all go and v-v-vlog the whole trip!' Abby and Jessie gestured frantically at them from across the room – they obviously had the same idea. A Girls Can Vlog trip, the perfect thing to take their channel to the next level, liked they'd discussed in their resolutions video.

'Guys, you should attach Go Pro cameras to your helmets!' said Morgan excitedly, forgetting to lower her voice. 'They record the most amazing downhill footage and you can even monitor how fast you're going!'

But as Miss Piercy continued to talk about the trip, Hermione's heart sank. Full parental approval was required, and with her mum in her current mood, she didn't rate her chances. Plus, the more she thought about it, the more she worried that she wasn't exactly cut out for racing down an icy slope . . . especially not with a camera in hand! But still – a trip away would be so much fun . . .

Have you read the first fantastic book in the
GIRLS CAN VLOG series?

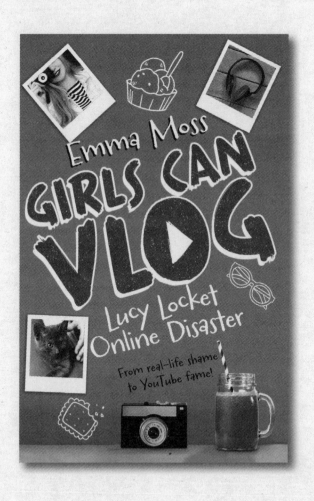

Collect them all!

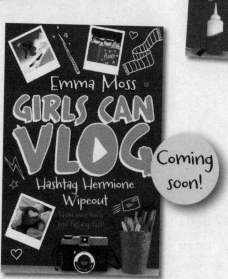

Coming soon!